"Now you know the whole truth. I'm only sorry you got hurt."

"I'm *not* hurt," she said, more for her benefit than his.

"I am."

The whispered words sent a shiver through her. She wanted to believe him so much that it caused a dull ache, a longing she couldn't explain.

Caleb approached, standing between her and the door. His shoulders sloped, and for an instant he appeared as deeply affected as she. "I know you don't want to hear it, but I promised myself I'd be totally honest when I came back this time. About everything."

"You're right—I don't." She looked everywhere but at Caleb. She didn't dare.

"I just want to say that if circumstances were different, I believe we might have had something between us." A pained silence followed. "At least, *I* felt it."

GEORGIANA DANIELS

resides in the beautiful mountains of Arizona with her super-generous husband and three talented daughters. She graduated from Northern Arizona University with a bachelor's degree in public relations and now has the privilege of homeschooling by day and wrestling with the keyboard by night. She enjoys sharing God's love through fiction, and is exceedingly thankful for her own happily ever after.

A Daughter's Redemption

Georgiana Daniels

Love Inspired

Recycling programs
for this product may
not exist in your area.

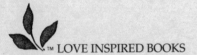 ™ LOVE INSPIRED BOOKS

ISBN-13: 978-0-373-87792-8

A DAUGHTER'S REDEMPTION

Copyright © 2013 by Georgiana Daniels

www.LoveInspiredBooks.com

Printed in U.S.A.

Be kind to one another, tenderhearted,
forgiving each other, just as God in Christ
also has forgiven you.
—*Ephesians* 4:32

To my husband, Troy, who works extra hard
to afford me the freedom to follow my calling.
You amaze me!

Acknowledgments

A very special thanks to my agent
Tamela Hancock Murray
and my editor Emily Rodmell
for believing in this newbie! To crit buds
Betsy St. Amant and Erica Vetsch, for the prodding,
stretching and love that went into the critiques.
To Gina Conroy, for cheering me all the way
to the finish line.

Chapter One

If the rest of the property was in the same sad condition as the front porch with its missing rails and bowed floorboards, Robyn Warner would be in Pine Hollow, Arizona, far longer than she'd anticipated. She wheeled her suitcase over the flagstone walkway and paused at the foot of her father's home to absorb the onslaught of memories.

It wasn't too late to turn around and hand the keys back to the lawyer managing her father's estate, though the sad huddle of cabins hardly qualified as such. What had once been a cozy mountain resort now looked pitiable and highly susceptible to a stiff wind. Her father certainly hadn't done her any favors by willing the property to her, but after more than a dozen years of silence, she was glad to be remembered at all.

Gravel crunched near cabin two—Robyn's favorite during her summer vacation stays as a child. A man in work pants and a paint-splattered T-shirt meandered out from between the ramshackle buildings. "Can I help you? It's easy to get lost out here."

"It certainly looks different than I remember, but this is the right place." She shaded her eyes to get a better look at the man who was tall and muscular without being imposing. He was the most clean-cut maintenance man she'd ever seen—and a nice contrast to the surfers with sand in their hair she was used to back at the surf shop she managed in California. She propped up the suitcase. "I'm Robyn Warner. And you are?"

"Caleb." He gestured toward the road. "Pine Hollow Resort is on the other side of the wash, about five miles down. Are you sure that's not where you were headed?"

"I'm here to check out…" She caught herself before referring to Lakeside Cabins as hers. "I'm staying here. Dan Dawson was my dad." She fished the keys from her pocket and held them up. "I'll just let myself in."

The handyman scrutinized her as though assessing her legitimacy, much the same way her half siblings, Brad and Abby, had during the funeral last week. Gauging her motives and questioning her right to be there. Her right to grieve.

He swiped his brow with his arm and slid on a pair of sunglasses. "No one told me you were coming or I'd have cleared out."

"If it makes you feel better, the lawyer didn't tell me about you, either." She offered a tentative smile. "Or maybe he did, and I was still in shock." She recalled her conversation with Phil Harding, who'd upended her world when he contacted her after the funeral and said Lakeside Cabins was hers, though all her father's personal items would go to Brad and Abby. "Do you work here?"

Caleb shuffled the paintbrush from one hand to the other. "I've been fixing Lakeside up, but I can leave if you'd rather have the place to yourself." His tone held a hard edge.

"Not at all. I'll be glad to have your help. It looks like we have a lot of work to do." Though she didn't have a clue how to pay him. She made a mental note to ask the lawyer if there were provisions of some kind. After taking an unpaid leave from the surf shop, she was living on savings—meager ones, at that. "The sooner Lakeside is all fixed up, the sooner I can sell it."

"It could take a while." Caleb's neck bobbed with a hard swallow, as though he wanted to say more. His sunglasses kept her from further reading his expression, though it was becoming clear she made him uncomfortable.

"With the two of us working together, it'll speed things along." She smiled, hoping to defrost his stoic demeanor. Having an easy rapport with the handyman would make the work and the memories of Lakeside less painful. "Either way, I'll be here as long as it takes. But please, keep doing whatever you were doing." She gestured toward cabin two. "Every little bit helps."

Caleb offered a curt nod before he crossed back over the clearing and disappeared behind the small building.

Wind moaned through the trees, sending birds skittering from the branches. Robyn rubbed a chill from her arms. Something about being in the quiet space where her father lived so many years without her, so many years without birthdays and Christmases and simple phone calls, left her unsettled. She wished she'd disregarded her mother's repeated warnings to leave her dad and his family alone, that she was no longer welcome to visit. She should have at least tried to make peace. Now she'd never have the chance.

Robyn drew a fortifying breath before inserting the key into the lock. She worked the key and turned the knob several times, but it refused to budge. Before she could shimmy it out and try again, the phone in her pocket rang. Her thumb hovered over the button until she finally worked up the courage to answer. "Abby, how are you?"

"As good as can be expected. Listen, Brad and I haven't finished moving everything out yet, so he wants to make sure you don't take the armoire in the bedroom." Abby's voice had matured and no longer resembled the giggly pre-teen Robyn remembered.

She plugged her ear to drown out the wind. "I haven't even been inside yet. Trust me, I wouldn't have a way to move the furniture out even if I wanted to." She glanced at the rental car she'd put on her painfully thin credit card.

"Sorry, I know it's awkward." A long pause stretched over the line. "Brad just wants me to remind you that the furniture and personal belongings are ours. We'll be back to get them."

"I haven't forgotten." She swallowed her sadness. She and Abby had once been close until the argument that drove Robyn away from Pine Hollow—an argument with their father about how she felt less important than his other children. Lately she'd begun to crave the closeness of a real family, and now that circumstances had brought her back, she'd do whatever it took to restore her relationship with Brad and Abby. To find some sort of normalcy.

"Good. We wouldn't want any misunderstandings."

"Abby, I would never take what doesn't belong to me." She fingered the cross on her necklace and prayed for wisdom. "Maybe when you come out for the furniture we can have dinner. We have a lot of catching up to do."

Silence pulsed between them until Abby cleared her throat. "I'm not sure that's a good idea. We're still shaken up."

So was she. The tragedy of losing a parent—even an estranged one—was overwhelming.

"I mean, why would Dad leave Lakeside Cabins to you? No offense, but you haven't exactly been around."

The words stung with truth, and her face heated from the rejection. "I understand. Give me a call when you're ready to come by."

The line went dead.

"Is everything okay?"

She whipped around, disconcerted. "Caleb, you startled me." She scanned his face to figure out how much he'd overheard. His expression remained neutral behind the sunglasses, which left her even more flustered.

"I heard voices and thought maybe you were talking to someone."

"I was. It was a private conversation." She jammed the phone into her pocket.

"I was only trying to help." Caleb held up his hands in surrender, then turned and stalked off.

"Wait." She scrambled down the stairs, her sandals slapping the wood. Exactly why she chased after the maintenance man or even cared what he thought, she'd have to reason out later. "I didn't mean to snap at you."

Caleb angled toward her, his mouth quirked. The masculine scent of turpentine and hard work drifted off him, and for some reason, it wasn't entirely unpleasant. "Apology accepted." His somber tone seemed to say otherwise.

Robyn ran her hand through her hair, snarled from the wind. "Really—I'm sorry. I'm not exactly great company right now after what happened to my dad. I'm normally easy to get along with—you'll see when we fix this place up, and before you know it I'll be long gone."

Judging from Caleb's formidable posture and the twitch of his jaw, her departure wouldn't be soon enough.

Caleb stormed into the office of Harding and Company and bypassed the receptionist. Without knocking, he entered the office of Phil Harding, attorney-at-law. "Why didn't you tell me she was coming?"

Phil tapped the keys on his computer without missing a stroke. "Almost finished. Then we can talk."

"You should've at least given me a heads-up." He pulled the door closed with a thud. "Didn't you think I might need that bit of information?"

All the way from the outskirts of Pine Hollow, he had rehearsed the diatribe he wanted to unleash on his so-called friend. But none of his imagined scenarios included Phil calmly pecking away at the keyboard.

Phil closed the program and spun around in his leather chair. "I presume you're talking about Robyn."

"Who else?" He dropped onto the cushioned seat, and if he dirtied the upholstery with his paint-stained pants, so be it.

"What'd she do?"

"She showed up." Simply arriving at the cabins was enough to infuse him with a jolt of reality. What originally seemed like a brilliant way to fulfill his promise quickly turned into the single worst idea he'd ever had the moment Robyn, with her sun-bleached hair and sorrow-filled eyes, told him she was Dan's daughter.

"Look, Caleb, I realize it's a little awkward."

"You think?" He blew out a frustrated breath. "I tried to play it cool in front of her, but you have no idea what that was like."

Phil removed his wire-rimmed glasses and wiped them with a handkerchief. In a placating tone, he resumed. "I can't control every variable. Did it occur to you I might have other projects I'm working on?"

He pushed out of the chair. "A phone call, Phil. That's all I needed."

"She came in only an hour ago and asked for the keys. I wasn't expecting her back in town so soon." Phil steepled his fingers and assessed Caleb with a concerned look. "I did mean to call you when I got the chance, but you're right. I should've made sure you were aware."

The admission took Caleb's boiling blood down to a simmer. He gripped the back of the chair and stole a few deep breaths. It wasn't entirely Phil's fault. The unease that chewed on Caleb day after endless day had fueled the tirade. "I shouldn't be this upset."

"You're under a lot of stress. It happens." Phil came around the desk and palmed Caleb's shoulder. "I know you want to do penance or something by fixing up Dan's place, but if you ask me, you should be home. You need time to recover."

"That's what the chief told me, but it was code for 'stay out of the police station until we decide whether or not you can keep your badge.' Waiting for the decision is killing me." A knot formed in his windpipe, cutting off his air. This was not the time to have a meltdown.

"It's procedure. Don't take it personally. You need to let go of the guilt."

"My career is personal. It's the one thing…" He stopped short of telling Phil it was the only reason his own father had accepted him and that carrying on the family tradition had come to mean everything after his father's untimely death while on active duty. Caleb took a moment to compose himself. "Bottom line is that I made a promise I intend to keep." He flinched at the unbidden memory of crouching over Dan on the sidewalk after he'd been hit by the reckless teen Caleb had been chasing. The older man had pleaded for help, and Caleb had looked into the dying man's eyes and promised to do everything in his power to make it all right—a promise he wasn't able to keep. At least not during the few remaining moments Dan was alive. Caleb swallowed the emotions that threatened to choke him. "I couldn't help him then, but fixing up his property is what I can do now. This isn't about me or guilt. It's all about keeping my promise to Dan."

"If that's what you need, fine. Don't worry about Robyn. She seems friendly enough, but it's not like you have to talk to her. Of course, she'll probably have some ideas about what she'd like to have done, but you pretty much have a handle on the situation."

"Her being friendly has nothing to do with how she'll feel once she knows."

"There are some things you can't control." Phil rubbed his temple. "I know you're worried about what happened, but I've looked into the station's policy myself. Legally speaking, you're not necessarily in the wrong. There's room for an officer to use discretion when a subject flees."

Too bad Caleb's discretion had led to Dan's death—the worst tragedy in Pine Hollow's history.

At the time, he was sure pursuing Aaron Dirkson was the right decision. How could he have known the teen would take the corner too fast and hit Dan? Still, he was compelled to defend himself. "The kid was a troublemaker. I was sure he'd been drinking that day, and I had a responsibility to get him off the street."

"You don't have to convince me." Phil met Caleb with a soft look. "You may not have been officially cleared, but I have faith Aaron will be convicted, and you'll be back patrolling the streets before you know it. In the meantime, give Robyn the benefit of the doubt. She might be surprisingly understanding."

"I don't want to borrow trouble." Caleb rubbed the back of his neck to ease the building tension. "I know I need to tell her, but as soon as I do she'll probably make me quit working on the cabins. I have to have something to keep me busy while I wait to hear whether or not I have a career left."

"Giving up your work at Lakeside wouldn't be the worst

thing in the world." Phil's gentle tone burned like acid on an open wound.

Knowing his decision cost a man's life slammed his conscience as much as if he'd been the one behind the wheel. How would he quiet the guilt if he couldn't keep his promise to do everything he could for Dan? It was all he had left, especially if they stripped his badge.

"You don't understand." He paused for a deep breath. "I made a promise to a dying man, and if fixing up the cabins is all I can do to keep it, then that's what I'm doing." He gripped the back of the chair, knuckles white, and locked gazes with Phil. "Just give me a few days and let me tell her in my own way."

The intercom buzzed. "Yeah, Marge."

"Robyn Warner on the line for you."

Phil shot a reassuring glance. "I'll take it." He picked up the phone. "Robyn, what can I do for you?" His forehead wrinkled. "Stuck? You haven't been inside yet?"

Caleb shook his head as a warning.

"No problem. I'll send Caleb out there right away." The lawyer disconnected. "She needs help. The door's stuck."

"I gathered that." He narrowed his eyes. "Look, I'll figure out a way to talk to her. In the meantime, whatever you do, don't tell her who I am."

The sight of Robyn on the porch swing sent a fresh rush of adrenaline through Caleb. Though he'd driven all the way out to the lake with his sunglasses off, he slid them on before approaching her.

"Thank you for coming back." The swing creaked as Robyn stood. Her wide and honest eyes, the color of robin eggs, perfectly mirrored her name. "I tried several times, but I couldn't get the door open. So I hung out down at the dock for a while hoping you'd come back. Then when you didn't, I called Phil. I hope you don't mind."

"Phil gave me a key for the side door." Caleb motioned for her to follow.

The suitcase Robyn tugged clunked down the stairs. Without asking, Caleb grabbed the luggage handle from her and carried the suitcase over the stony ground to the side entrance.

"You don't have to do that." Robyn quickstepped to keep up with him. Her unassuming manner was refreshing, and for an instant, his mood lightened.

He caught himself before accidentally engaging in conversation. He yearned for the days when he could speak without measuring his words. When he could behave as though there wasn't a millstone crushing his conscience. When he could wake without counting how many lives he'd destroyed.

In the distance, sunlight glinted off the lake and the chatter of birds filled the pine-scented air. The property had potential, and Caleb was determined to help maximize its value before he revealed his identity and Robyn booted him out.

He fished the key from his pocket and inserted it into the lock.

"Wait." Robyn grabbed his forearm. "If you don't mind, I'd…" She left her comment hanging.

Caleb stopped and dared to really look at her. Wavy, golden hair flowed freely down her back. Her shorts were faded and frayed. She wore sandals so flimsy they could hardly be considered footwear. Robyn Warner seemed to have just stepped off the beach, and the look suited her.

"I'd like to go in alone." Her vulnerable gaze peeled back Caleb's layers, softening his heart toward the grieving woman. "I need a few minutes to take it all in, if that even makes sense."

"Of course. I should've thought of that." He backed away from the door, allowing the key to dangle in the lock. "I won't need those while you're here."

Robyn's eyes moistened. "I appreciate your understanding."

He nodded and started toward the front of the house.

"Wait," Robyn called. "How well did you know him?"

The question sent a nervous tingle down his back. He refused to turn around. "Not very well."

"It's just that I'd like to talk to someone." Robyn paused as though silently asking him to face her. "It helps, you know?"

The woman obviously had no clue who she was speaking to or she'd kick him off the grounds. Ignoring her was going to be a problem. How could he? She was Dan's daughter. "I'm sorry about your dad."

"I didn't realize how much I'd miss him."

Slowly, Caleb turned. "It hurts to lose someone you love." He, more than anyone, knew how hard the unexpected loss of a parent was. And some days were decidedly harder than others.

"Most people don't think I did."

"Did what?"

"Love him." She cast her gaze to the rocky ground. "It doesn't matter now."

"I'm sure it'll take a while to adjust." He closed the gap between them, rifling through his thoughts for something appropriate to say. "In the meantime, you'll be hanging out here. It's the perfect place to get away."

"That, it is." Robyn's eyes locked onto him, as though seeing through the mask he'd donned every day since the accident. "What about you? Do you sometimes need to get away from it all?"

"I can't," he blurted before he could censor himself.

"Why not?"

Caleb shook his head and walked away. Answering the question was impossible. There was no way to explain to Robyn Warner that the one thing he wanted to get away from was the one thing he never could.

Himself.

Chapter Two

It wasn't the memories inside the house that assaulted Robyn; it was the lack of them.

The night closed in, trapping her inside her father's home. She moved from what had once been the check-in desk to the kitchen, from the living area to the bedroom, searching for evidence, no matter how minute, that her dad had loved her. She would have happily settled for a picture of them together, the clay handprint she'd made when she was nine or even the stash of clothes she'd left behind. But by the time she dropped to the couch to sleep, she'd come up with nothing.

It didn't help that Brad and Abby had already stripped the home of all the valuables, including everything electronic or sentimental. Even the edibles were gone, except for an old can of coffee. It left Robyn with entirely too much time to think.

When the sun cracked the horizon, she was itching to head to town, but she knew it'd be a while before Pine Hollow woke up. Instead, she took time to pray and devour the half-eaten candy bar she'd found at the bottom of her purse. After that, she dressed and ran a brush through her hair.

Her outlook for the day buoyed, and she shuffled into

her sandals and meandered down the winding path that cut through the forest toward the lake. The water had always been her favorite place to clear her head when she was a kid, feeling left out after her father married and had two more children—a family that lived with him, when she only had a few weeks during the summer.

Caleb sat at the water's edge on a boulder, chucking pebbles. He didn't turn, but from the hunch of his shoulders as she approached, he knew she was there.

"You're here early." Robyn rubbed her arms, wishing she had a better line. If she wasn't so starved for conversation, she would've hightailed it back to the house. She wasn't used to spending time alone, nor was she used to having to prod someone to talk. If Caleb didn't open up, working together would be unbearable.

"It's a good place to think and pray." Caleb focused on the sparkling water, never sparing her a glance.

She smiled at the thought of Caleb being a praying man. It was a refreshing difference from the guys Robyn worked with at the beach. She hooked her thumbs through her belt loops, refusing to take the hint and leave. It was her property, after all. "You don't talk much, do you?"

"Only when I need to."

"All the time or just for me?" She lightened her tone and willed him to let his guard down.

"Everyone, lately." Finally, he glanced up at her. He appeared gentle, despite his square-cut jaw and military-precise haircut. "Did you need something?"

A friend—not that she'd ever admit it out loud to someone she'd just met. Her throat constricted as she shook her head.

Caleb tossed the rest of the pebbles to the ground and stood. Slowly, he advanced. "If you need something, you can ask." Behind his shades, it was hard to tell what he was thinking. He stood close—too close—and the smell of his crisp aftershave made her lose track of her thoughts.

She risked a smile. "I'm just trying to figure out where to start. It's hard to come back after all these years and sort through—" she motioned toward the cabins, unsure exactly what she was sorting through besides her tangled emotions "—things."

"Doesn't sound like anything I can help with, so while you sort through 'things,' I need to head back to town." Caleb started up the path. "I'll be back later."

"Didn't you just come from town?"

"The hardware store called. My lumber order is in, plus I need more paint."

She hurried up the path after him. "Shouldn't painting be last on the list? Let's walk the property and decide what else needs to be done."

"Make your list, and I'll look it over." His stride widened.

"I don't know how you're getting paid, but I'm sure it's safe to assume you won't be working indefinitely so we might as well focus on the big stuff, like the floorboards on the porch and replacing the window on cabin one."

Caleb halted. He opened his mouth but seemed to think better of saying what was on his mind. "The lumber I ordered *is* for the porch. We can talk about what you'd like done when I get back."

"I want to come with you." Robyn lifted her chin.

"Like you said, there's a lot to do. Maybe you should concentrate on making a list for me." A line formed between his eyebrows, as though he was trying to read her.

"As long as you're going to town, I'm coming, too. I have a vested interest in picking out colors and whatnot. Besides, I have my own list to deal with."

Caleb's morning whiskers rasped like sandpaper when

he rubbed them. "All you have to do is tell me what you want and I'll pick it up while I'm there."

"Can you pick up a Realtor?" She challenged him with a raised eyebrow.

His mouth tightened. "Fine, you can come. But I doubt anyone is open."

"They will be soon enough." She walked quickly and prayed for him to soften. "When we get back, we can do a walk-through. There's a leak under the kitchen sink, and the porcelain in the tub is cracked. I think we can get most of the repairs knocked out in a few weeks."

"We?" Caleb's tone took on a gruff edge. He stopped and faced her.

She smiled broadly. "I thought I mentioned that yesterday. The job will get done much faster if we work together."

"No offense, but I tend to work better alone." He pinched the bridge of his nose and blew out a long, exasperated breath.

"We don't have to stand side by side." She tossed a casual glance toward the cabins. "There's plenty to keep us both busy. It seems like the whole property has been neglected for a while." She bit back further comment, not wanting to offend Caleb over the job he'd done—or not done—so far. "How'd you come to work out here anyway?"

"Long story." He took off up the hill.

She quickened her steps to keep up. "I'm curious."

"You know what they say about curiosity."

"If you don't want to talk about you, then maybe you can tell me more about my dad. Since you worked for him, you probably know more about him than you think. It's been a long time since I saw him. Of course, you probably knew that." She hoped he'd tell her more without her having to spell out every detail of their estrangement.

"I wouldn't assume too much if I were you." His lips

held the barest trace of a smile, or perhaps it was more akin to a frown. Either way, he lost the gritty expression he'd clung to from the moment she'd introduced herself.

"I guess I'd just like to know what my dad said about me." If anything. Robyn was nearly out of breath when they emerged from the pine trees into the clearing. What had once been lush with grass and a flowerbed was now hard-packed dirt overrun with weeds. Why hadn't Brad and Abby done more to help their dad? After all, by growing up here full-time they'd been close to him in a way Robyn never could be.

"I talked to Dan a few times. We ran into each other every now and then at church. I wasn't someone he confided in." A look that Robyn supposed was sympathy crossed his face. His jaw flexed. "I'm sorry I don't know more, but I only came here to work…after."

After. She knew he meant after the accident.

An unexpected swell of grief surged in her chest. The rapid change of emotions she'd experienced since her father's death was new and would take some getting used to.

She ambled toward Caleb's black truck, hiding her watery eyes. "After all this time away from here, I'm surprised how much I miss him." She stopped herself from opening up to Caleb any further. Finding out he hadn't actually worked for her dad made him a virtual stranger. Even her mom, as free-spirited as she was, warned Robyn against being so open and friendly. Still, Caleb's presence was calming, and he seemed safe enough.

He shook his head regretfully. "One thing I do know is that your dad was a good man. Everyone misses him. You can't go anywhere in town without someone mentioning Dan."

Robyn gripped the door handle, trying to move past

the sadness pressing against her chest. It was time for her to think about logistics, rather than dwell on her feelings. "Do you mind if I ask how you're getting paid? I suppose that's something I'll need to take care of now that I'm here."

He hesitated. "Don't worry. It's being handled."

That was all Robyn needed to know—about that topic, anyway. She still had questions, myriad questions. Like what Caleb knew that he wasn't saying. Or why her dad willed the run-down cabins to her after a twelve-year estrangement. But most of all she was desperate to know if he'd forgiven her or simply done what he felt was his duty.

Questions she'd likely never have answers to, no matter how hard she searched and prayed.

The drive to town was pure torture.

Rather than ride in silence, Robyn asked Caleb about himself. He tried to be vague, but she was impossible to ignore, especially with a scent that reminded him of an ocean breeze wafting off her. Even worse, her eyes sparkled with a quiet hope whenever she mentioned Dan. Caleb imagined Robyn was highly likable when she wasn't walking through a tragedy, which reminded him that being her friend was one hundred percent out of the question.

"I hear Ginger's the best Realtor in town." He parked his truck curbside and let it idle.

Robyn peered out the window at the sign on the door. "Ginger Hanson?"

"You know her?" He shifted in his seat, wondering who else Robyn knew. Who else had the potential to rip the cover right off him? Not that he enjoyed withholding the entire truth from Robyn but he had his own issues to deal with before purposely heaping more sorrow on a woman he'd just met.

"I spent a few weeks every summer with my dad when

I was a kid." Robyn turned to him, a full smile illuminating her features. "Ginger and I were together every day at Lakeside Cabins, checking in guests and cleaning rooms. We lost touch after I stopped coming." Her gaze shifted to her sandaled feet. "I didn't see her at Dad's services."

Caleb tightened his grip on the steering wheel at the mention of Dan's funeral. In order not to upset half the town, he'd opted not to go. "I can pick you up when I'm finished at the hardware store."

"It looks like Ginger's office hasn't opened yet. We can come back later."

There she went with *we* again. The word sent prickles down his back. He had to figure out a way to tell her who he was. He'd prefer waiting until after the cabins were in salable condition so she wouldn't force him to leave before the job was done, but Robyn's insistence on working with him would make that next to impossible.

Against his better judgment, he let her tag along.

Joe's Home and Hardware was already alive with activity. For decades, it'd been a meeting spot for contractors, do-it-yourselfers and retirees. Despite Caleb's work hours on the police force, he made it a point to stop by on occasion, if for no other reason than to get a beat on the town.

Caleb whipped a cap out of the glove compartment and pulled it low over his eyes before entering the store. If he made it out with paint and his lumber order without someone giving him away, he'd consider it mission accomplished.

Cold stares and whispers greeted him inside, and people turned their backs when he walked by. Dan Dawson had been part of the daily gathering at the hardware store, and no doubt his buddies missed him.

"Why don't you pick out the paint, and I'll head back

to get the lumber." Caleb broke away from Robyn before she had a chance to protest.

He inhaled the comforting smell of sawdust. He'd spent his college summers on various job sites back when he thought he wanted to be a contractor instead of a cop. Though he'd eventually chosen a different path, he was thankful to have the skills he needed now to do repair work at Lakeside.

"'Morning, Caleb." Old Joe, the store's owner, eyed him.

"I came to pick up my order." Caleb pulled the receipt from his pocket and handed it over the counter. His eyes darted around the store, searching for Robyn. He didn't want to imagine the scene if she wandered back and one of the regulars asked why she was there with Caleb Sloane.

Joe's arthritic fingers riffled through papers in a file bin. The small store hadn't quite caught up to the computer age. "Here it is. I'll have one of the guys load it for you."

"I'm parked out front." Caleb tucked the receipt inside his wallet, his eyes making another sweep of the store. No sign of Robyn. The tension in his gut ratcheted up another notch. A few more minutes and they'd be out of there.

Joe's stare closed in on Caleb, years of history passing between them in seconds. "Still working out at Dan's?"

"Doing my best."

"Just not the same around here without Dan. He always had time for a cup of coffee and a story or two. He was a good ol' boy." Joe leaned away from the counter, his comment stabbing Caleb in the gut. "I don't suppose your best really makes up for it."

With nothing left to say, Caleb headed for the paint department.

Robyn shuffled through paint chips like a hand of cards. "I like lighter colors, but it might stand out too much in the forest." She locked into his gaze, causing his heart to react in ways it had no right to. "Maybe we should stick with brown. What do you think?"

"I was going to keep it the same color Dan chose, but it's up to you." He snuck a glance around the area for workers or customers who might know who Robyn was. So far, everyone but Old Joe seemed content to ignore him. "Why don't you choose, and I'll finish up in here."

"We'll stick with dark brown then." She stashed the fan of paint chips on the display. "I probably shouldn't worry over the details so much. It's just that I really want to get this right. It's not all about selling and the money. As much as I hate to admit it, this is my last chance to do something for him."

Mine, too. Caleb steeled his emotions, blocking out every runaway memory that threatened to surface. He held out his keys. "Go ahead and wait in the truck. I'll pay."

"I thought that was my responsibility." She narrowed her eyes, as though not quite believing his motives were pure.

"I told you that it's all been handled." He jingled the keys in front of her, briefly wondering if he was doing the wise thing by using his own savings. He wanted to do right by Dan, who'd obviously fallen on hard times before his death, but it wasn't like his bank account was anything to brag on. "I'll be right out."

Robyn stuffed her hands into her pockets, the corners of her mouth tilting in what would be a teasing gesture under any other circumstances. "Are you giving me the brush-off? I have to warn you—" she leaned in close "—I'm not that easy to get rid of."

His heart skidded. The fact that she wasn't going to be easy to get rid of—and that her shimmering eyes and easy-going confidence were already wearing down his protective wall—was precisely the problem.

Chapter Three

Robyn spent the better part of the next morning trying not to notice Caleb, who was clad in a fitted white T-shirt and baggy jeans. As he fixed the leak under the kitchen sink, he finally appeared to relax and carry his end of the conversation, though he still seemed reluctant to venture beyond talk about plumbing and floorboards. She wondered if Brad and Abby had gotten to him with negative comments about her before she arrived.

Since she hadn't found Ginger Hanson the day before, she headed into town while Caleb sawed wood for the porch. She made a mental note to swing by the grocery store since she'd had to skimp by on stale crackers and tuna she'd found in a cupboard. At least Brad and Abby had left something.

Seeing Ginger for the first time brought back a rush of memories, as did the windy stroll through the town square where the women stopped at a coffee cart.

Iced mochas in hand, Ginger launched into the conversation as though not even a year had passed, much less a decade. "The news about your dad was a shock. I didn't find out until I got back from vacation. I was hoping to see

you, but I figured you'd be gone by the time I got back."
She gently laid her hand on Robyn's arm.

"It looks like I'll be stuck here for a while." As they
walked, Robyn sipped her mocha and soaked in the sights
of the lazy, secluded town. The Tasty Pastry, the ice cream
parlor and the pizza joint hadn't changed a bit. Across the
road sat a new bookstore and a youth center to complete the
town square. Several people milled about the courthouse
lawn, despite the storm looming overhead. She'd forgotten
how quickly the weather changed during monsoon season.

"Stuck? How so?" Ginger's jet-black hair fluttered in
the wind.

"Believe it or not, Dad left the cabins to me, and they're
in pretty bad shape. I was surprised to be named in the
will. I figured everything would go to Brad and Abby
since I haven't seen or heard from any of them in over a
decade. Actually, I think they were more surprised than I
was." Robyn hadn't a clue why her father had picked her
over the children he'd raised at Lakeside with his wife. As
a real family. She refused to dwell on the past or the fact
she'd faced some of the hardest years of her life without a
father and with the constant reminder she was the product
of an illegitimate relationship.

Ginger's gaze penetrated Robyn's thoughts. "He was
your father, too. Of course he'd leave you something."

"Still surprising. Anyway, I was sad to see how they'd
been let go. I remember Lakeside being alive with guests,
but now it's like a ghost town." Robyn veered down a
path that bisected the courthouse lawn. "When I saw Abby
and Brad at the service, they treated me like an outcast. I
thought maybe we'd all grown up enough to be civil. But
I was wrong. Really wrong." She missed the secrets and
fun they'd shared growing up. While she hadn't expected
to pick up where they left off, she also hadn't anticipated

the cold indifference. How would she even begin to restore their relationship? It was a long shot, but she had to try. She didn't want to go through her entire life without her family.

Ginger sat on an empty bench at the edge of the town square. "They never did change. I mean, they have to be pushing thirty years old."

"I think Brad just turned twenty-six."

"Still, they act like kids. Spoiled—both of them. No loss for Pine Hollow when they moved to Phoenix. Your dad was always the nicest man, but those two took after their mom. They seemed to get even worse after Marilyn died."

Dad had married Marilyn Bell, the hometown sweetheart, who'd hounded Robyn for the smallest mistakes. Treating her like an outsider in her father's home, even though she was there before Marilyn. Robyn squirmed. "I thought they were the perfect family, that they didn't need me or even have room for me in their lives."

"His wife may not have come to terms with him having a daughter from a previous relationship, but that's not your fault. I'm sure Dan never felt like there was no room for you in the family."

Robyn settled herself on the bench and tried to block out the memories that said otherwise. "I'm sorry I didn't call. Once my mother told me that I wasn't welcome to come back, I did my best to forget all about Pine Hollow." She spoke past the knot forming in her throat, remembering the Lord's promise to be a father to the fatherless. "That should never have included you. After I left, Mom and I spent years drifting from one beach to the next, and I never really felt settled."

"As much as I like the beach, I can't imagine what it must've been like not to have a place to call home." Ginger's mouth slid into an easy grin. "But as for our friendship, thank the Lord for new beginnings."

"I'm glad I found you." She was thankful for another chance with her childhood friend.

Ginger held up her phone. "Once I have your number, you won't be able to get rid of me. Now, am I right in guessing you'd like me to sell the property? It's going to take a while for the estate to settle. I can look at it anytime, but we won't be able to list it yet. You'll have to get an appraisal and whatnot first, but it'll give us more time together—at least once I get back from a conference I have to attend in Phoenix next week."

"I took an indefinite leave from my job, so I'm staying until it's sold." Even though a few nights spent in her father's home had left her more disquieted than ever, especially since she hadn't found any clues about her dad's feelings for her.

"Have you already found a contractor? I know a few people."

"The lawyer hired someone, but I don't think he's a contractor. More like a handyman." Robyn's pulse jumped as she remembered the scent of Caleb's cologne and the way he held the doors open for her every time they entered one of the cabins. He was a refreshing change from her surfer buddies who'd never heard the word *chivalry.* She chucked her cup into the trash can next to the bench.

"Hopefully it takes months to fix up the cabins." Ginger grinned. "I want to keep you here as long as possible."

"That'd be nice, but sooner or later I'll have to get back to work—back to something close to normal, whatever that is." She waved to Mrs. Jones, who stood at the door of the bakery.

"I don't believe my eyes. Is that Robyn Warner?" Mrs. Jones called out. "You make sure to stop in and see me."

Her heart warmed, remembering the lazy afternoons

she and Ginger had shared with chocolate on their cheeks, shirts caked in powder from the donuts. "You bet I will."

A few moments passed. Ginger shifted awkwardly on the bench until she finally spoke. "I felt awful when I heard about your dad. This town isn't the same without him." She clutched her chest. "The whole situation is unbelievable. And the fact that the kid who did it walked away with minor injuries… I'm just glad the case will be a slam dunk."

Robyn's chest pounded in time with a low rumble of thunder. "It's hard to think about it. I keep imagining the worst."

"I won't pretend I understand what you're going through, but try to remember that your dad's at peace now." Ginger patted Robyn's hand again, and shook her head slowly. "But I still can't believe they didn't fire the cop."

"Cop?" She sat straighter and searched her memory for any mention of a police officer. "What am I missing? What are you talking about?"

"The cop who was involved." Ginger pulled an umbrella out of her leather tote. "I don't know the details, but the whole town is in an uproar. I've never seen people take sides like this."

Robyn swiped away the first drops of rain that fell like pinpricks from the sky. "Back up a second. I thought a teenage driver hit my dad. No one mentioned an officer."

Ginger's eyes rounded, and she opened her umbrella with a snap. "Oh, no. Maybe— I don't want to be the one to say. And of course, all my information is secondhand. Like I said, I was out of town when it happened."

"Please, tell me what you know." She fingered the cross on her necklace. Maybe it was better not to hear the details.

"It was a chase. From what I heard, the kid ran a stoplight, and a cop tried to pull him over. When the car refused to stop, the cop followed him through town, rather than letting him go. The kid was trying to outrun the police when he swerved and—" Ginger winced "—people are saying the officer violated a no-pursuit policy the department has."

Robyn's stomach clamped. Her mouth dried, and her erratic heartbeat drowned out the thunder. She licked her lips, taking a moment to order her thoughts. "Do you mean to tell me the whole thing was preventable?"

Ginger's eyes filled with sorrow. "Some people think it was and that the kid wouldn't have spun out of control if he wasn't being chased."

"Tell me what else you've heard." Robyn grasped Ginger's arm.

"I guess the officer is on suspension."

"Someone has to hold him accountable. You're sure he wasn't fired?"

"I'm sure he will be. Or...I don't know. I've been out of town so much I haven't heard the details."

Robyn stood and slung her purse over her shoulder, ignoring the fat drops of rain that pelted her skin. "It looks like I have a few questions that need to be answered. Whatever it takes, I'm going to get to the bottom of this."

Spending time with Robyn had been worse than Caleb imagined. Way worse. More than once he'd found himself smiling and engaging in conversation before he remembered why he couldn't. His relief was palpable when she left for town—until Phil showed up and tried to take him to lunch.

"I have to finish cutting these boards before it rains. I don't have time to stop." He glanced toward a cabin, remembering Robyn's contagious grin when they'd walked the grounds.

"Since you're working like a madman, I assume you told her."

Caleb remained silent.

"Wait, you mean you haven't said anything yet?" Phil's question hit like a sucker punch.

"I'm trying to keep to myself." He was failing miserably, but trying. He focused on a squirrel scampering up a nearby pine tree.

"Just get it out in the open. I'm telling you, if it wasn't for—you know—I think you would hit it off. She's cute."

Cute was an understatement Caleb wasn't willing to acknowledge. "That was a low blow." He slid his protective goggles over his eyes and powered up the circular saw.

"Sorry. I wasn't thinking." Phil's voice cut over the grating whine of the blade.

Caleb powered down. "I don't want to talk about her—or any of this. Everything was fine when I was here alone, but this is getting ridiculous."

"So stop."

It sounded simple enough, but he had a promise to keep. A little hammering and painting was the least he could do, and he wasn't about to give it up, though it didn't minimize the stress of dealing with Dan's daughter. If the situation were different, he might actually enjoy her company and the seemingly endless stream of friendly conversation. The interest sparkling in her eyes that he knew he had no right to return. The more time they spent together, the tighter he had to guard himself—at least until he devised a way to reveal the truth.

Phil pushed his glasses up the bridge of his nose. "Forget all this for a while. Let's grab some lunch."

"You should've called first."

"I tried. You didn't answer."

"Leave a message."

"I've left three. Look, man, you can't hide out forever. People don't hate you if that's what you're thinking."

"I never said that, but let's be honest. People in town are getting pretty ugly." Caleb fixed his eyes on the pile of lumber at his feet. "Now if you don't mind, I have a porch to rebuild. I have to keep busy until the review board hearing. You have no idea what it's like to have your job and your reputation hanging in the balance." It was a crushing weight that never left him room to breathe or the freedom to rest. The review board's recommendation to the chief would determine his future.

"Working yourself to death isn't going to make time speed up. Maybe what you need is to forgive yourself." Phil checked his cell phone. "There's still time to grab a bite to eat before my next appointment. Come on. It'll do you good, and it wouldn't hurt your cause to be seen out and about. Let people see that you have nothing to hide."

"I *don't* have anything to hide. And I don't want to keep my job based on PR moves that came from my lawyer friend." Caleb removed the goggles from his head. He worked the elastic with nervous fingers. "My career means everything to me. I have to keep it based on merit, based on the review board's belief I did the right thing. Any other reason isn't good enough." Not for him and not for his father's memory.

"It's all about perception." Phil gestured with his hands. "Face it, doing work out here makes you look bad. Like you believe you were wrong."

"I don't care what it looks like. I'm here because I promised Dan I'd do everything in my power to help. I couldn't do it at the scene—" he choked down the familiar knot in his throat "—so I'm doing it here."

Phil leaned against the sawhorse Caleb set up in the clearing between the cabins. "I'm telling you what the perception is. It's important that you know. Now come to town with me."

"Lunch won't solve anything." It wouldn't help him forget his career was in jeopardy. Or forget Robyn's hopeful smile when she offered him coffee—the only thing she'd found in the cupboard. No, stopping long enough to eat was a bad idea.

"Will I at least see you at church this week?"

A vise gripped Caleb's stomach. For the past few Sundays, he'd done his best to keep a comfortable distance from the church—and Dan's friends inside of it. "Maybe."

"Hang in there." Phil clapped Caleb on the back.

The silence after Phil drove away was short-lived. Robyn's rental car swerved into the dirt lot, kicking up a dust cloud. She barreled out and slammed the door.

Caleb searched her face for what had caused this uncharacteristic level of emotion. "You're back early. Need help bringing in the groceries?"

Robyn stopped short of the table, arms folded. "It's unbelievable."

"What's wrong?" His instinct was to offer her a shoulder and tell her everything would work out. Instead, he stayed rooted behind the sawhorse and hoped his expression didn't betray his worry over what she may have discovered in town. "Didn't you find Ginger?"

"I'm not upset over Ginger, and I never made it to the store." Robyn's words were pinched, her eyes fiery. "She told me more about my father's accident."

Adrenaline slammed through his veins. He'd known this moment was coming, but there was nothing he could've done to prepare. He shot up a silent prayer and wheeled in a large breath. "There's always more to the story."

"You'd better believe there is." Robyn fisted her hand on her hip, and a gust of wind stirred her hair. She swept the strands away from her reddening cheeks. "Evidently, the whole situation was preventable."

He swallowed, then nodded for her to continue.

"I was under the impression that a teenage driver hit my dad on the side of the road and that was it." She covered her mouth and took several moments to collect herself. "But Ginger told me that a police officer was chasing him. That despite the station's policy, the cop pursued. He endangered the public, and look what happened."

Caleb stood tall despite the dread that pummeled him. It was time to take the consequences and trust the Lord to handle the outcome. There was no fear in truth, of that he was convinced. So why did his conscience burn with every word from Robyn's mouth?

"As it turns out, the cop hasn't even been fired. If it wasn't for this officer's bad judgment, my dad would still be alive."

His heart wrung with a bitter mixture of guilt and relief. Obviously no one had told her who he was, but it was only a matter of time—time that would run out quickly in a town the size of Pine Hollow. An apology hummed in his chest, trying to pressure its way out. He resisted, unsure he could live with the confession. Certain he would implode without it.

"I don't know why this had to happen. It probably sounds ludicrous, but I planned on making things right with my dad one day. Now I never can." Robyn's face turned to stone. "But I intend to find out who did this, who ruined our lives. And believe me—he will pay." She brushed away a lone tear, her mouth drawn tight.

Caleb stood, dread pressing against his rib cage like an anvil. He wiped the sweat beading on his forehead and waited for his nerves to calm. How could he ever admit to Robyn that the person she was looking for, the one who destroyed her chance to reconcile with her father, was him?

Chapter Four

Caleb's face blanched, and his throat bobbed with a swallow. He sat on a nearby stump. "I'm sorry."

"Not at all." Robyn waved him off, regretting her outburst. She drew a deep breath to compose herself. "I didn't mean to sound so hysterical. It's just that…" She glanced toward the tree line at the sound of an approaching vehicle. A silver truck rounded the bend—one she recognized from the funeral. Her mouth went dry. "It's Brad."

"He was here before, clearing the place out." Caleb stood, a guarded expression in his eyes. The truck stopped abruptly.

She smoothed the hem of her shirt and braced herself. She'd been praying for a chance to talk to Brad and Abby before they left town, before they all parted ways again—this time for good. Now was her chance, and she hoped she appeared calmer than she felt. "You've met my half brother?"

"Not exactly." Caleb's jaw flexed when Brad shut off the engine. "He didn't say much when he was here, other than telling me he knew exactly what was on the property. His meaning was implied."

Robyn cringed, wondering how bad their encounter was.

"Why's he here? There's not much left except heavy furniture, and he'd need help for that." She schooled her features as Brad slammed the truck door and closed the gap between them. "How are you?"

"Fine." He whipped off his shades. "Where's the rest of the paperwork?"

"What paperwork?" She stepped back.

Brad walked toward her, then halted when he noticed Caleb off to the side. "Don't play dumb. Dad's files. What'd you do with them?" He nailed her with his gaze and raised a pointed eyebrow.

"I haven't seen any files." She forced a smile, despite the uneasiness growing inside her. She chose her words carefully, rather than slipping back into big-sister mode and demanding to know what had gotten into him. "Come inside, and I'll get us some coffee."

He brushed past. "I need to have a look around."

Robyn started to follow, but Caleb gently tugged her elbow. She turned toward him. "I'm going to help my brother." Even though she didn't have a clue what he was looking for, and didn't appreciate his attitude. But more than anything, she wanted to make a connection with him while she could. She'd already learned life didn't give a person unlimited time to repair relationships.

Caleb shook his head, his gaze trailing Brad. "Let him go. Something's not right."

Anxiety wormed through her as she watched her half brother storm into the house. Maybe if she helped, he'd be less agitated. "You don't understand." She pulled away from Caleb, vaguely aware his hand had been steadying her. She started toward the house. "It might be my only chance."

"Your only chance to what?" Caleb's gentle tone reeled her back.

"To talk to him." It pricked her conscience to know she'd waited so long to reconcile that she was down to chasing her angry brother, who clearly didn't want to be bothered. She closed her eyes to clarify her thoughts. "I know it sounds ridiculous, but if I don't go after him now, that might be it."

Caleb held up his hands. "I won't stand in your way. Be careful."

The warning lingered in her head as she made her way up the steps. What did Caleb know that she didn't? She reached for the door at the same time Brad opened it. He pounded down the steps.

She stumbled out of his way. "Did you find what you were looking for?"

Brad wheeled to face her, his stale breath assaulting her. "Does it look like I did?"

Frustrated, she counted to three before answering. "You didn't have time to find anything. Let me help—"

"You can help by telling me what you did with the rest of Dad's files. There had to have been more." Brad raked his hand through his dark blond hair.

Robyn walked down the steps into the clearing, thankful for Caleb's presence. This wasn't the little brother she remembered—mischievous, but kind. This seemed like someone else altogether. "I haven't seen any files or paperwork, but I'll keep my eyes open. How about I call you if I find them?" She pulled her phone out of her pocket.

"Like that's going to happen. I know you took them." Brad fisted his hand and made a sudden move toward her.

Caleb cut him off. "Calm down, bud. There's no need to accuse Robyn. Let's talk this out."

Brad pointed at Caleb's chest. "This is none of your business."

"I'm making it my business." Caleb stood firm, arms crossed.

Silence shrouded the clearing long enough for Robyn to swallow the nervousness rising in her throat. She shot up a quick prayer. "I'm only trying to help."

Brad's jaw ticked, and even with Caleb between them, Robyn could feel the anger coursing through her brother. "I don't know why Dad left this place to you, but one thing is sure—you don't deserve it." He pointed at her. "According to the will, everything on this property that's not nailed down belongs to me and Abby. If I find out you're holding back…" He let his threat hang as he turned and made for his truck.

Robyn exhaled, hands trembling. "I've never seen him like this." She looked at Caleb, drinking in his cool demeanor that reassured her during this unexpected encounter. "I don't know what I would have done if you hadn't been here. I mean, I'm sure he would've calmed down eventually. He's probably still upset about Dad—we all are."

"Don't make excuses for him." Caleb retreated behind the sawhorse.

"I'm only saying that he wouldn't act that way if it wasn't for the circumstances." She searched his eyes for understanding.

"His behavior isn't excusable." Caleb pulled out his measuring tape.

"You're right." She shook her head, trying to get her mind around what just happened. "Thanks for stepping in."

"Anyone would." He marked the lumber and didn't meet her eye.

"I think most people don't like to get involved."

"You might want to stay away from him."

"I can't. He has every right to come here and get our

father's belongings. I hate to admit it, but he made me uneasy." Robyn rubbed a chill from her arms, then dipped her head to lock into Caleb's gaze. "I hope you're here when he comes back."

She wouldn't be saying that if she knew who he was, and the realization stung.

What was coming over him? He couldn't deny the surge of protectiveness that blasted through him when Brad appeared to threaten Robyn. To believe it had anything to do with the way she looked at him with those hopeful blue eyes would only further derail his plans to reveal his identity.

Why hadn't he unburdened himself of the truth when he had the chance? The moment he'd arrived at Lakeside the confession stuck in his chest like wood glue. And bringing it up now while Robyn expressed her gratitude after the encounter with Brad didn't seem right, either.

"He almost completely ignored me at Dad's services, but I could understand that. Then after we found out Lakeside went to me, he stopped talking altogether. But this—I don't know what to make of what happened just now. Maybe I should call Abby and see what she thinks." She reached into her pocket and pulled out her phone.

"Who's Abby?" Caleb leaned on the sawhorse, gauging Robyn's emotions.

Tears glittered in her eyes, but she maintained her composure. "My half sister. She's close to Brad, so maybe she can tell me what's going on and what paperwork he's looking for."

That must've been the woman who'd come with Brad when they hauled out most of the furniture. Since he hadn't been to the funeral, he didn't know who was who in terms of the family. Thankfully, they didn't know him, either.

Caleb measured the lumber propped on the sawhorse, his mind working overtime to focus on anything but Robyn's sweet demeanor. It wouldn't do him any good to get distracted from his mission. "If that's what you want."

"What do you mean by that?"

"Exactly what I said." He marked the cut line and hoped it was right.

"If you have something to tell me, spit it out."

Boy did he, but judging by the tremor in her voice and the red splotches in her cheeks, she was still traumatized. Adding to it seemed cruel. Neither could he stand here and pretend he'd be around the next time her crazy brother showed up—or pretend he was innocent.

"Just keep your guard up. He doesn't seem like the kind of guy who'll let family loyalty keep him from getting whatever he's after." Caleb set down the pencil and measuring tape, exhaled and began to pack his tools. Though there was still a good four hours of daylight left, he was ready to shut down. He needed quiet time to think. To pray. To dig up enough courage to come clean and hope Robyn let him continue to work at Lakeside, though judging by her outburst before Brad showed up, he may as well be packing his tools for good.

Then what would happen to her? He'd seen guys like Brad before—who used intimidation or whatever means necessary to get their way. Men who picked on women were cowards—and needed to be watched.

"You're right—again. I don't really know him anymore." Robyn shoved her phone back into her pocket. "My mom's been telling me for years that I'm too trusting."

No joke. He could be an ax murderer, and she'd still be chatting away like they were having a picnic. After the way she made excuses for her brother, Brad could very well cheat her out of the property Dan had specifically wanted her to have. And while Caleb's promise was to Dan, he didn't want to see all his hard work benefit Brad.

"Are you done for the day?" Robyn watched him. "I was hoping you'd show me how to patch the walls in the house. I saw the drywall kit, and I'd like to get started."

Caleb wiped the sweat from his forehead. The breeze rustled the tall grass in the clearing, cooling his face. "Tomorrow."

She folded her arms. "You're sure cutting out early."

That's right—she thought he was hired help. If he were being paid, instead of funding the whole project himself and laboring for free, it *would* be early. Realizing the futility of resisting her, Caleb nodded. He whisked past her toward the main house, determined to finish quickly.

"Just give me a few minutes. If you show me how to do it, I can finish the job. Trust me, I want to help so we can get this place on the market."

"Anxious to leave?" He refused to turn around and let her see the spark of interest he was sure was in his eyes. Every encounter with Robyn made it harder to smother the attraction, and he spent an enormous amount of energy to keep from looking at her. To stay quiet and aloof. He held the door open and allowed her to pass.

She paused a beat before answering. "There are a lot of memories here, and some of them I'd rather not relive. Besides, I have a job and a life I need to get back to."

"Understandable." He turned over an empty paint bucket and sat near the part of the wall needing repair. Leaving this job to her wasn't a good idea, but it *was* her house. "Are you sure you want to start the walls on your own?"

"I'm perfectly competent, if that's what you're worried about."

Caleb dared to look into Robyn's eyes. His heart jack-hammered in his chest, and his mouth dried like the Arizona desert. What was it about her that had his head turned inside out? In the few short days since they'd met, he found his thoughts veered toward Robyn more often than not, and he looked forward to seeing her even though he knew with unshakable certainty this couldn't end well.

"So show me what to do." She picked up a putty knife and smiled.

"If you wait until tomorrow, I can do it."

"It's only right for me to fix it since I'm the one who put it there." Robyn's smile waned as she set down the knife. "You know how this hole got here? One day Abby and I were practicing for the softball tournament and whack!" She chuckled. "Instead of fixing it, Dad moved the high-back chair in front of it. As you can see, he wasn't really handy."

"Did you get in trouble?"

She tilted her head, lips tight. "Not at first. We were younger, and Dad hardly ever got riled up. But when my stepmom saw it—" she exhaled before continuing "—she let me have it. Not Abby, of course. Just me." She cast her gaze to the floor. "I was ten when that happened, when I started to realize that she only tolerated my summer visits, but I wasn't really welcome."

"Sorry to hear that."

Robyn straightened and waved him off. "That was a long time ago. I've had a great life—it's just that coming back here reminds me of the hard parts." She stepped away and gazed out the window. "I don't even know why I'm telling you this. I get chatty when I'm nervous."

Poor woman must be nervous all the time.

"How about you? Are you from Pine Hollow?"

"I'm a transplant from Flagstaff." He tried to keep a brisk tone. The less questions, the better—at least until the time was right.

"I know all about being a transplant. But Brad and Abby—they had a rock-solid childhood here. It's no wonder he's not really happy about me taking over Lakeside."

Talk about an understatement. Who knew what Brad might have done had Caleb not been around? He hated to judge, but Brad set off every internal alarm he had. "When do you suppose he'll be back?"

Robyn shrugged. "Hopefully not until he calms down. I just want to be part of the family again. After being away for so long, I know it won't be easy, but I'm starting to realize family is the only thing that matters." She turned over another empty paint bucket and sat next to him. "You're right. I really don't want to do this today. Mostly I wanted to keep my mind off what happened. I guess I'm more shaken up than I thought."

And with good reason.

In that moment, he made a decision he hoped he wouldn't regret. Leaving Robyn alone to face her brother wasn't acceptable. If that meant he had to keep to himself a few more days until the ruckus blew over, he'd do it. Only then would he tell her who he was—and what he'd done. After all, the best way to keep his promise to Dan was not only to restore the property but to look out for his daughter.

Chapter Five

Raindrops streaked the windshield and pattered against the roof of the truck. Caleb parked in front of The Tasty Pastry, then reached behind the seat to grab an umbrella. But before he could offer it to Robyn, she hopped out. Caleb pocketed his keys and followed.

"I forgot how much I love monsoon season." She turned her palms upward.

Caleb fed the parking meter, then glanced around for anyone who might have noticed him with Robyn. He refused to be caught off guard, and while coming to town was taking a big risk, he hadn't been able to tell Robyn no when she asked to ride along. In fact, he was starting to realize the word *no* wasn't in her vocabulary not only when she wanted something but also when asked for help. He liked that about her, even if half the time it drove him crazy.

"What time should I meet you back here?" Her gauzy shirt billowed in the breeze and made her eyes sparkle.

The sight of her slender form and dimpled cheek distracted him. It had distracted him all morning while they worked on patching the walls. He'd found himself sneaking glances at her far too often when he should have been focusing on the repairs. He prayed he'd have enough time to finish before it was necessary to tell her who he was.

"Caleb, did you hear me?"

He snapped back to the present. "An hour."

"Sounds great." She waved at someone down the road. "There's Ginger. See you," she called over her shoulder.

He ducked inside The Tasty Pastry, where the smell of fresh bread and coffee greeted him. The tables sat empty, and only the owner occupied the tiny shop.

"Caleb Sloane, you've been away too long." Ida Jones came around the counter and smothered him with a maternal hug.

"I haven't been away, just laying low." He stepped back and perused the display case.

"That's plain silly." She grabbed a towel and wiped the counter. "I know half the town is having a conniption, but they need to get over it. You didn't do anything wrong, and if you ask me, we're all better off with Aaron Dirkson behind bars so he can't hurt anyone else." She sighed. "Like Dan. Anyway, you did what you thought was right." She fisted her hand on her ample hip. "You know I once caught Aaron trying to set fire to the trash in the Dumpster out back? That's the least of what he was into, from what I hear."

And Caleb knew she'd heard plenty. "I appreciate your vote of confidence, Mrs. Jones."

"Someone told me they're going to let people have their say when the review board meets. I plan to give them a piece of my mind." With a flair, she pulled her apron strings tighter. "Now when is that, again?"

A fresh wave of anxiety punched him at the mention of the hearing—and with it the possibility of losing his job. "They pushed the date back. It'll be a month from yesterday." Every day more nerve-racking than the one before.

It's in Your hands, Lord.

Despite his mistake in judgment, God still had a plan. He had to keep on believing it or he'd go berserk. Yet living like he believed it proved to be another matter.

"You don't have a thing to worry about. Maybe folks will settle down by then."

Or get more worked up. No, he had to stop thinking that way. Keep praying. Keep believing. Keep working at Lakeside. "It's good to know people like you still have a good opinion of me." He glanced over his shoulder to make sure no one was on their way into the shop, then leaned on the counter. "What have you heard about Brad Dawson?"

A frown creased Mrs. Jones's brow. "It depends. What do you want to know?"

"For starters, what he's normally like. I had an... encounter with him."

Mrs. Jones edged closer and lowered her voice. "You wouldn't be the first person. I'm not one to gossip, so anything I tell you is common knowledge."

Caleb nodded for her to continue.

"He was the sweetest little freckle-faced kid you ever saw. Dan used to bring him in all the time, along with his sister Abby. She was younger and quieter and always followed his lead. But when he became a teenager and his mom was ill, he changed—and not for the better."

"Did he have a temper?"

Mrs. Jones kneaded a towel as she spoke. "He had the shortest fuse this side of Phoenix. Then there was the drugs and alcohol, and it's no secret he's got money troubles." She shook her head. "Reminds me a lot of Aaron Dirkson."

Reminded Caleb of what his life might have been, had a worker at the recreation center he frequented not prayed some sense into him. "So it's safe to assume Brad is trouble."

"Unless he's changed. People do, you know." She set down the towel. "The town practically breathed a sigh of relief when he moved to Phoenix. That must've been about the time you came to Pine Hollow. Oh, dear, I should've done more praying for that boy."

"Thanks for the heads-up. I have a feeling I'll be seeing more of him." Caleb drew back and pointed to the glass case. "I'll take all the chocolate donuts and croissants you've got."

"You always know how to make my day." She grinned, appearing ready to pinch his cheeks if she got the chance. The bell above the door tinkled, and she waved before turning back to Caleb. "Are you taking these to the youth center to share with the kids?"

"'Course he is. He can't eat those. He's got to keep an eye on his figure." Phil clapped Caleb on the shoulder. "I was wondering what happened to you. Expected you next door ten minutes ago, but I knew where to find you." He winked at Mrs. Jones.

"I didn't want to come back for the first time empty-handed." Caleb's heart lifted at the thought of the youth center he'd started last year. Seeing how small-town life was affecting the teens of Pine Hollow and the activities they'd try to alleviate boredom, he felt compelled to take action. Securing grants for funding and a location and finding volunteers had been a monumental task. One that was well worth the effort.

"As long as you're back, I don't think the kids care." Phil peeled off his glasses, fogged them and wiped the lenses.

Mrs. Jones peeked up from behind the case. "See, we all agree you should hang around more, Caleb."

"It's hard to stay away, but for now I'm checking in." He buried his hands inside his pockets. "I've got my work cut out for me at Lakeside." At least until Brad was no longer a threat, he came clean with Robyn and she told him to leave. Despite his fervent prayers last night, he couldn't see any other way for the scenario to play out—and it irritated him to realize how much he wanted a different ending. It'd only been a few days, but already Robyn had burrowed into his daily routine and most of his thoughts.

And if he wasn't mistaken, the feeling was mutual.

Caleb had stood up for her. A warm sensation filled Robyn when she remembered his protective stance, the way he'd taken charge of the situation. Would anyone else have done the same? None of the men she knew had the courage, or if they did, she hadn't noticed. In fact, Caleb was the first man who'd turned her head in years, despite how carefully guarded he seemed.

"Are you paying attention?" Ginger nudged her.

Robyn tried to appear interested in picking out blinds, but with yesterday's confrontation with Brad, not to mention her rapidly shrinking bank account, window coverings ranked low on her list of priorities. "There's so much to choose from."

Ginger peered over her shoulder as she leafed through the sample book. "I'll bet these would look great in the front room."

"Are you sure we have to do this?"

"Window treatments make all the difference to the look and feel of a room. And without them, the light shines straight in and highlights the problem areas. You're the one who mentioned how bad it looked." Ginger ran her finger down a column of measurements and checked it against the notes Robyn had made. "Besides, it's only for the main house. The cabins can stay as they are."

Only for the main house. Casual words for someone who actually had money to her name, but for Robyn, *only* the main house meant wiping out her bank account. As it was, she'd had to turn in the rental car, and the refrigerator was nearly empty. She had to make what little money there was last until she got paid again. She made a mental note to ask Phil what provisions existed for renovating.

People meandered around Joe's Home and Hardware, chatting with one another as though they had no business but to catch up on the day's events. Between the full mugs and fun-filled laughter, it was hard to tell if this was a hardware store or a coffee club. Had her dad been part of this group, hanging out with his friends?

"These seem to be the most reasonably priced." Ginger tapped the page, then frowned. "Is something bothering you?"

"Brad came out to Lakeside yesterday, and we had a run-in. I can't stop thinking about it."

Ginger pulled up a seat, the legs of the chair screeching against the concrete floor. "What did he want?"

"He said he was missing some of Dad's paperwork, but he wouldn't give details." Robyn leaned against the sample book and rubbed her forehead, though the real pain was in her heart. "I have a feeling that getting on his good side will be harder than I thought."

"Are you sure you want to?"

Robyn sat next to her friend. "I know it sounds crazy but yes. Now that I have a chance, I'm taking it."

Ginger raised one highly suspicious eyebrow before her features softened. "I won't pretend to understand, but you and I can have a long talk when I get back from my conference."

Robyn stood. She twisted the wand on the display blinds. Open, shut, open, shut. "I'm sure what happened yesterday was a fluke. Let's get the saleslady and finish up. I'm supposed to meet with the handyman soon."

The salesclerk came over and drew up the order. Robyn handed the woman her debit card, hoping it wasn't declined. She prayed there would be enough money made on the sale of the property to cover what was still owed along with the expenses she was incurring.

After they finished, they strolled out of the store. A rainbow hung over Pine Hollow, and the scent of rain permeated the air.

Ginger grabbed Robyn's forearm. "Don't look now."

Robyn looked. Abby sauntered out of a boutique like she owned the sidewalk, nose tilted skyward. She waved and hoped her half sister was in a better mood than their brother. "Hi, Abby. I thought you had headed home to Phoenix for a while. What brings you back so soon?"

Abby straightened her collar. "Business." The clipped word made her cringe.

"I'll leave you two alone." Ginger backed away to peruse a window display.

Robyn forced a smile and prayed for the right words. "Ginger and I were ordering new blinds. I think they'll look good in the house."

Abby responded with a simper. Where was the sister she'd played with as a kid, the one who splashed around in the lake with her, made mud pies and whispered secrets late into the night? A sister—a whole family, really—was the only thing Robyn wanted. What could she say to bring peace?

"Abby, look—why don't we call a truce? I don't know what you and Brad still have against me after all these years, but I want to get along."

"You really don't know?" Abby's eyes narrowed.

"The past is the past."

"And sometimes the past bleeds over." The venom in Abby's words struck their target, and after a few moments, her features softened, if only a little. "But even now, I have my reasons."

She tried to ignore the attention they drew from the other pedestrians. "Tell me. I'll do whatever I can to make it right."

For the first time, Abby's composure was shaken. "You can't make it right. Like I said on the phone the other day, there was no reason for my father to leave Lakeside Cabins to you. That was my home growing up. You left, and yet you're rewarded?" Her pitch rose with intensity. "I don't think so."

"I may have walked out, but I was sixteen years old and full of emotions I couldn't get a grip on. But you'll never know how much it hurt to be told that no one wanted me to come back."

Abby huffed. "I don't know anything about that, but it serves you right. My parents had nothing but trouble whenever the subject of you came up, and it really hurt our family."

At least you had one. Robyn swallowed the comment in order to focus on what was important now. "Look, I don't know why Dad left the property to me, either, but it's the only hope I have that he actually cared about me. I want to get along with you—and with Brad. It's not like we have to be friends, but can we at least not be enemies?"

A dark cloud passed over the sun, and the breeze stilled, as though all of Pine Hollow was pausing to hear Abby's reply. "There is one thing you can do."

Robyn's heart fluttered with fresh hope. She'd do whatever it took to make peace with her sister, no matter the cost. "Tell me."

"There's a hearing coming up, for the police officer who was involved in the accident." Abby's eyes turned to stone. "Brad and I are going to have our say and hopefully get that person off the force. You can prepare a statement, too. After everything that's happened, you owe it to Dad to speak up."

Anger bubbled inside her at the mention of the cop, but she'd never been one for vengeance. "I'm not sure what to say."

"Say yes." Abby's mouth tipped up at the corners. "It's the least you can do."

Chapter Six

The more time Robyn spent with Caleb, the harder it was to resist the growing attraction. What good would it do to get to know him better when she'd soon be gone? She craved a loving, stable relationship, but she knew this couldn't be it—even though she caught him sneaking glances at her and sharing more frequent smiles. Life on the road with Mom had taught her not to get too attached.

An ache pierced her back, a by-product of hunching over the porch's loose floorboards all morning. She sat tall and stretched.

"Are you ready for a break?" Caleb's rugged voice startled her from her thoughts.

"Only if you are. I can keep going until we're done."

He set aside the nail gun and rubbed his face. "You go on ahead. I need to keep working. I hear there's a storm coming, and I'd like to have more finished before it hits." His biceps drew the fabric of his T-shirt taut as he reached for another plank.

Robyn's arms felt like noodles. She'd mistakenly thought she could easily handle these tasks after spending the past year moving surfboards and boxes at the shop. But that was nothing compared to the heavy-duty work over the past several days—when Caleb didn't stop her and handle the tasks himself. She stood and tugged at his arm. "Come on, you deserve a break. I insist."

He glanced at the sky, then back at the hole in the porch. "I'll take a short one. Let me grab my food from the truck."

The half sandwich she'd saved from breakfast was still on the counter inside. After paying for the blinds, she'd had just enough money to buy a loaf of bread, peanut butter and jelly. She still had one more paycheck from the surf shop coming, but after that she'd have to break out the credit card. Hopefully the renovations would be done soon so Ginger could list the property.

She unwrapped the sandwich and met Caleb outside. "Mind if we walk? I need to stretch." A path cut between the cabins and led to the forest. She motioned for him to follow.

Judging by the way he eyed the pile of lumber, he was anxious to finish the job, but he finally consented, the same way he had every day this week. Each time he opened up a little more, but he remained more guarded than anyone she'd ever known. She'd never met the strong, silent type before and she enjoyed the challenge of drawing him into conversation.

Grass and wildflowers covered the path until it was hardly detectable and certainly nothing like she remembered. How many times had she walked this trail with Abby when they were looking to ditch their housekeeping duties? Surely, dozens.

She savored the first morsel, unsure how long it would be until she could stock up at the grocery store. "Do you have another job lined up after this?" The question was met with an extended pause, which she suspected meant he didn't.

"I don't know what God has in store for me." He took a large bite of his twelve-inch sub.

She broke off a corner of bread and tossed it to a bird near a thicket. "I know that feeling all too well." The acute sensation of being unsettled haunted her after leaving Pine Hollow and being told not to return. Would she ever have a real home? She swallowed the rest of her sandwich and wished for a glass of milk. "I don't know about you, but I've found it's much easier to talk about trusting Him than actually doing it."

"That, it is. Nice to talk to someone who understands." Caleb finished the last of his sandwich in silence, then scattered the remaining crumbs for the birds. He pivoted. "Hate to rush, but I need to get busy. You take all the time you need."

A breeze whispered through the trees. Robyn closed her eyes and inhaled deeply, treasuring the moment. "You seem more anxious to finish Lakeside than I am."

"There's a lot to be done." He kicked a pinecone along the path.

"Don't remind me." She fell into step beside him, determined to enjoy their break. "Does your family live in Pine Hollow, too?" She hooked her thumbs through her belt loops and trained her eyes on the chipmunks scampering around a bush.

"No siblings. My mom lives in Tucson."

"Do you see her often?" She stopped to pick a wild-flower, then realized he hadn't answered. "I didn't mean to bring on the inquisition. I know you like your privacy."

He offered a thin smile. "Once a month—I get to Tucson as often as I can. She occasionally visits here during the summer."

"I thought you were from Flagstaff."

"When I moved from Flagstaff so did Mom. That was

about six years ago. The minute I got to Pine Hollow, I knew I wanted to make it my home."

"It's amazing you knew so quickly." She smiled, thankful for the cracks in his wall, cracks that had shown themselves more and more often. She was also thankful for his company. She was used to customers, coworkers and friends surrounding her. Since being at Lakeside, her interactions had been severely limited, except for the guy who installed the blinds—and another encounter with Brad.

He'd come out again two days ago, loaded a few more pieces of furniture and asked about the mysterious papers. Slightly less gruff than the last time, he still gave the distinct impression he wanted nothing to do with her. She hadn't even had a chance to tell him she'd agreed to side with them at the hearing. Thankfully Caleb had hovered close by, appearing ready to intervene if Brad so much as raised a pinky.

They emerged in the clearing, and Robyn was almost sorry to have to get back to work. "How'd you know you wanted to stay?"

"For the most part, Pine Hollow is a great place to live. Slow pace. Quiet. I always figured I'd have a family and retire here."

The idea of remaining in one place, grounded and stable, sparked wistfulness inside her. "You're a long way from retirement."

He mumbled, "Hope so."

Robyn climbed the steps, and when Caleb moved toward the loose floorboards, she tugged his elbow and pulled him to the porch swing. The swing creaked when she sat. He eased down next to her—close enough to brush her arm and send a shiver down her back. Close enough to smell his aftershave, subtle and understated, just like he was. Close enough to hear the soft rhythm of his breaths.

And he didn't move away.

"I take it Pine Hollow is a little too small for your taste?" His voice carried a hint of resignation. He offered a soft shoulder bump. "There have to be almost fifteen thousand people in town now."

"Oh, that many?" She smiled. "Even so, I never had the chance to make it my home."

"The beach is your home, then?" He looked at her with intensity.

"As much of one as I've ever had." She toed the floor and sent the swing into motion. "My mom moved us around a lot. I never had time to get attached to any one place." Or any one man. Remembering the parade of boyfriends her mother had dragged into their lives had been enough to make Robyn cautious when it came to relationships. She refused to repeat Mom's mistakes.

"Must've been hard."

"That's why I'd love to get settled somewhere. I just haven't found the right place."

Caleb planted his foot and stopped the swing. Locked into her gaze. "Why not here? Maybe that's why your dad left Lakeside to you."

She wished it were true. She tore away from his stare and surveyed the property. "Guess I'll never know. I have a feeling he made the will long ago and forgot to change it."

"Even so, this place is yours."

Robyn bit her lip, worry pooling inside her. Already she'd overspent, and more expenses lay ahead. "There's no way I could afford to keep Lakeside Cabins. If I understood Phil correctly, there's still a mortgage and property taxes. Selling it is my only choice."

"That's too bad." He kicked the swing into motion again, the gentle creak a comforting backdrop. "Just think of the possibilities. A little landscaping would transform the lot, and you could put a barbecue pit over there." He gestured to the edge of the clearing near a grove of trees.

Robyn laughed. "I'd love a barbecue pit, and while I'm at it, there's room for two more cabins. I'll hire the construction crew tomorrow." She nudged him playfully and then lingered closer to his side.

"Like I said, you never know what God has planned."

She hoped His plans included a family, people to anchor her. But for now she'd be happy to have Brad speak to her civilly. Daily, she prayed against the bitterness that tried to creep in. She refused to nurse a grudge. Instead, she chose to remember the little brother who'd skinned his knee in front of cabin one when he popped out to scare new guests. The kid who dunked her and Abby into the lake when they were sunbathing. The kid who curled up next to her when a storm knocked out the power.

Lord, help me to make peace. To continue to forgive, as I've been forgiven.

"You're awfully quiet." Caleb's low voice blended into the breeze.

Birdsong filled the air, and between the trees, she spied sunlight glinting off the lake. Everything reminded her of time spent here with Dad, yet nothing was the same. She shifted on the swing, breaking the easy rhythm. "I'd love for Lakeside to be filled with people again. Families, children. It's so quiet now. Too quiet." She swallowed the emotion rising in her throat. "I hope whoever buys it loves it as much as I did and makes it into something special."

"That's definitely on the prayer list."

Joy renewed her at the thought of Caleb praying for her need. As far as she knew, he was the first. "Since you're making a list, I have one more request."

"Shoot."

"There's a hearing coming up—you've probably heard

about it—and—" she paused to gather her thoughts "—I really want to see justice. For my dad."

Caleb stood too quickly, sending the porch swing flying. It'd be easier to tell her who he was, and get it over with. No more repairs, no more chitchat. No more Robyn.

Only with Brad likely to pop up at any moment, he hated leaving her vulnerable.

He'd have to tell her before the hearing, which gave him a few weeks to finish up so she could get a good price. Until then, he needed to keep his head down and his mouth shut.

"I'd better get busy before the storm hits." He mustered a smile, hoping to offset his abruptness.

Robyn stood. "I'm right beside you."

The rest of the day he worked faster and harder than before and restricted the conversation to floorboards, the upcoming roof repairs and the painting they could accomplish between storms. He didn't have time to play get-to-know-you, no matter how much he wanted to. Robyn needed him to stay focused, because once he was gone, no one else would take up her cause for free.

As much as he didn't want to admit it, he was no longer staying just to keep his promise to Dan or to keep himself busy until the hearing. At this point, he was staying for Robyn.

Chapter Seven

Robyn wandered down the path to the lake, inhaling the fresh scent of damp earth. She basked in the early-evening sun while considering her time at Lakeside. How quickly the past few weeks had passed while working with Caleb and how she didn't feel the same urgency to return to California as she did when she'd first arrived. There were still repairs to be done, but soon the property would be listed and she'd be packing.

All along she'd known this was coming, but what she didn't know was how hard it would be. In fact, the only reason for her to go back was a steady paycheck and a fully stocked kitchen. She took off her sandals, dangled her feet in the water and thought of Caleb. The man who'd noticed the almost-bare shelves in the main house and started to bring an extra sandwich every day. The man who said he'd pray for her. And without a doubt, the man who was now the reason she wanted to stay longer than she should.

At first she'd tried to dismiss it as her grief acting out or loneliness from being isolated at Lakeside, but she had to be honest. His quiet companionship had burrowed into a place in her heart she'd blocked off from everyone else, and she was falling for him—hard.

Robyn prayed for Caleb and prayed for her mom, who seemed more distressed by the day that she was at Lakeside. She even prayed for Brad and Abby and for peace between them all. But the more she prayed, the more unsettled she became about their situation. They hadn't come back to Lakeside, and they hadn't contacted her about the hearing. She'd hoped that working with them on a testimony would bridge the gap, but it hadn't been mentioned again.

A flock of ducks paddled by, and sunlight glistened across the gentle waves created by a small fishing boat. She glanced toward the boathouse near the dock, which gave her an idea.

Quickly, she rose and dusted off her pant legs and then picked through the weeds to reach the wooden shack that housed the water-sports equipment. The door groaned when she pushed it open. Cobwebs hung like muslin drapes across the ceiling, and a musty odor permeated the air.

Old, stained vests clung to the wall, along with an assortment of paddles and oars. A deflated pool raft took up most of the floor, and in the corner she spied the canoe. She wiggled around the equipment, making a mental note to clean out the storage area before Ginger listed the property, and then she grabbed the canoe. She rested the small boat against her shoulder and dragged it toward the door. Winded, she stopped for a few moments before venturing outside. A little tour on the water before settling down for the evening would clear her head—if she was able to haul the canoe to the edge of the dock.

"Need some help?" A deep voice echoed off the back of the boat.

She startled, losing her grip. A steadying hold tipped the craft upright. "You sure know how to sneak up on a girl. I thought you'd gone back to town."

"When I got to the turnoff, I remembered I left my phone." Caleb lifted the burden from her, allowing her to share only a fraction of the load.

She readjusted the weight and tugged the canoe to get them moving again. "Great time for a ride on the lake. It's been a stressful week." They came to the edge of the dock and lowered the canoe into the water.

"I'm sure you've had several stressful weeks. Anything you'd like to talk about?" Caleb focused on her, as though nothing else existed around them, and for a moment, she could imagine settling into his gentle care for the rest of her life.

She quickly shook off the notion, though still trapped in his gaze. "My brother, mostly." She motioned behind him. "I need to grab the oars."

"I'll do it." Caleb trotted up the hill and returned with the oars in hand. He hesitated, conflicting emotions crossing his features. "Mind if I join you?"

"I'd love it." She smiled broadly.

After setting the oars on the dock, he hopped into the canoe and reached up for her hand.

She placed her hand inside his, savoring the warmth of his skin and the firmness of his grip. In one swift motion, he took her by the waist and lowered her down. The canoe wobbled, and she laughed as they worked to catch their balance. Their gazes locked. She wheeled in a breath, keenly aware of his hand still on her waist.

Suddenly, he broke away and settled himself on the bench seat, which was filthy with years of neglect. "Shall we?" He offered her an oar, and after a few awkward strokes, they moved away from the dock. Caleb in the lead, taut muscles bunching beneath his gray T-shirt, they paddled out into the open water. When they reached the halfway point, he stopped and swung his legs around so they sat knee to knee. "Now what was it you were saying about your brother?"

Gently rocking in the canoe made her almost forget the strain she'd been feeling minutes ago. She laid the oar across her lap. "You've seen how Brad is. I know I've been gone a long time, but he's not at all the person I remember."

Caleb's face clouded over. "People change."

"I guess I don't know how to respond to him. A big part of the reason I came back to Pine Hollow was to reconnect with Brad and Abby, and I haven't made enough progress."

"Enough for what?"

She wiggled her toes in the water that seeped through the bottom and chided herself for not making sure her canoe was safe. "Enough to know that when this is all over—Lakeside is sold, Dad's affairs are in order—that we'll still keep in touch. See each other on holidays. That type of thing. Abby doesn't seem as set against me as Brad, but I was hoping for more."

"What do you think is getting in the way?"

"I wish I knew. Brad is still grieving—we all are, and maybe that's all that's going on with him. Everyone responds differently. Going forward maybe things won't be so strained—at least I hope not."

"You really care about them after what they put you through? Taking everything and being so hard on you?" Caleb cupped his hands together and scooped out water that pooled at their feet.

She started scooping water, too, though the floor quickly filled again. "They're family. I've learned the hard way that you don't always get second chances. I want to make the best of it, and if that means giving them the benefit of the doubt, or a little more leeway, then I'll do it."

Caleb's mouth tightened momentarily. "You're a good woman."

"Only because God helped me. It's that whole 'love endures all things' passage that gets me every time." She smiled, thankful to have overcome most of the negative feelings that hounded her for the past several years.

A speedboat hummed in the distance, disrupting the intimate quiet. Caleb picked up his feet, shoes dripping. "I suppose we should head back before we take on more water."

She laughed. "I should've made sure it was seaworthy."

"No, no—I don't mind wet socks." Caleb flashed a grin that stirred her soul and melted every last remaining defense. He reached out and squeezed her fingers, then raised his voice to outmatch the approaching speedboat. "Thanks for letting me come with you."

"Thanks for helping me get back to shore before we sink." She smiled and withdrew her hand. She gripped the oar tightly to keep from grabbing on to Caleb and never letting go.

"Whether we get back before we sink remains to be seen." He rose to turn around as the speedboat zoomed by and created a large wake.

The canoe swayed and bobbed, and Caleb's arms wheeled around to find balance. Robyn shrieked, then reached out and snatched a handful of shirt to steady him. He fell backward over the seat, landing halfway on her, halfway in the puddle on the floor. He erupted in laughter—the deepest, most sonorous laugh she'd ever heard. The sound warmed her heart, almost as fast as her arms warmed from his touch.

Caleb righted himself. "Not my most graceful moment."

"It's a good thing we're done working for the day."

His eyes sparkled, reflecting the lake—or maybe something deeper. He leaned close, tucked a wisp of hair behind her ear and caressed her cheek. "A little water never hurt anyone."

Neither did spending time with a handsome man, even if they'd have to go their separate ways. Only instead of accepting the situation as it was, her heart was starting to rip in half.

"I can't do it anymore." Caleb picked up his darts and stood in position. The clatter of air hockey pucks and teens ribbing one another inside the game room of the youth center failed to drown out the noise in his conscience.

Phil stepped aside. "Do what? Shoot darts?"

"Lakeside—I can't keep working at Lakeside." He hurled the dart and hit the bull's-eye.

"Great shot, Mr. Sloane!" Rocky Lopez called across the room. Kids clapped. From the general ruckus, it seemed they were glad to have Caleb around. At least the teens weren't taking sides against him like so many others in town were. He nodded and did his best to paste on a happy face. Or at least one that wasn't so grim.

"I thought things were going well?" Phil lined up for his shot.

"They were—when I was doing Robyn a favor by not telling her who I was. When I was protecting her from her brother. It's amazing she hasn't found out yet." He shook his head and took a seat at the table. "I don't know what's gotten into me."

"I do." Phil lowered his glasses and peered over the rims.

"That's the problem." Caleb fixed his stare on the darts in his hands. "I like her too much. I crossed the line."

"You're up." Phil switched him places.

"We're so close to finishing the cabins. I hate to bail on her now."

"So don't."

"You make it sound so simple."

"It is." Phil set his darts aside. "Tell her the truth."

He was desperate to come clean—except he had to find a replacement for himself first. Leaving her alone and defenseless against Brad wasn't an option. Neither was leaving her without help to finish the cabins. She was counting on the sale, and he was determined to do his part.

But he had to do it honestly.

"She might be more understanding than you think." Phil took his shot.

Like so many situations in his life, this one was completely out of his control. He knew what he had to do, and part of that was preparing for the worst.

That night, sleep was scarce. Peace ever scarcer. He armed himself with prayer, determined to do right by Robyn and trust God to handle the rest. But when he arrived at Lakeside the next morning, Robyn's eyes were red and she hiccupped a feeble hello.

"Sorry. It's been a rough morning." She dabbed her tears and flashed an incongruent smile. It was just like her, always trying to make the best of it. "I was thinking about Dad, and—well, never mind. Are you ready? It looks like it's going to rain. Hopefully we can get a lot done—"

"Don't apologize for your feelings." The porch creaked when he stepped toward her. Empathy overwhelmed him. Remembering that his mission today was to tell her everything, he fought the urge to gather her into his arms and ease her pain. He clenched his fists. "I know what it's like to lose a parent."

A quiver worked at her lips, and her eyes brimmed with unshed tears. "After all the years I spent away and everything that happened, I never knew it would be this hard." She covered her face with her hands, and before he could

stop himself, before he could think better of it, he pulled
her close to him and caressed the back of her head. The
feel of her silky hair beneath his fingertips was enough to
make him lose all logic. What was he doing? This wasn't
how he'd prayed for the situation to play out.

No matter how much he wanted to confess, to get it all
over with, he held back. Only a jerk would heap more sorrow onto a grieving woman.

Chapter Eight

The hug offered more than comfort, but Robyn hesitated to guess exactly what it meant. Especially since Caleb remained quiet most of the day, working with speed and concentration. Hopefully it was only due to the pending storm and not her emotional outburst.

The sun perched on the western horizon, obscured by dark clouds, and the moment they locked the last cabin, thunder rumbled. Robyn grazed her arms, remembering his gentle touch. "Do you need to get your tools inside before the storm hits?"

"There's a tarp in the shed. I meant to get it out earlier." He strode past her, around the back of the house. Thunder cracked in the distance, and a curtain of rain dropped over the clearing as she quickstepped to catch up. "Go ahead inside. I can take care of this," he called over his shoulder. "There's no use in both of us getting soaked."

"I don't mind helping." Any opportunity she had to be near him, she'd take. Oddly, she knew he felt the same even if he wasn't expressive. His thoughtfulness showed in the way he refused to allow her to do any heavy work, and he brought her meals without making her feel obligated. The way he gazed at her with an intensity that made her tremble.

Mud splattered her ankles as she navigated patches of weeds that covered the old trail behind the house. The path wound through a thicket of trees to a large wooden storage shed, covered in overgrown foliage. She'd forgotten all about it.

Caleb unlocked the dead bolt and ushered her inside. She brushed against him, keenly aware of his ruggedness and the way he stood over her in a protective stance. Aware of his square-cut jaw and his stoic presence that somehow brought comfort. Rain pattered against the tin roof, drowning out the bass drum beating inside her chest.

She couldn't recall ever having felt this way. No man had ever had the same effect as Caleb, and while it was exhilarating, it was also unnerving. Because now she'd started to kick around ideas of how she could stay in Pine Hollow—and it wasn't for the property.

Caleb angled past, smelling faintly of wet sawdust. He grabbed the tarp and unfurled it partway. "You grab that end and hold it over your head. I'll go out last so I can lock the shed."

The walls were lined with rusty tools hung on pegs, and camping paraphernalia occupied a large part of the room. Dusty boxes hid in the shadows, appearing to hold up the far wall. She picked her way across the shed to see if there was anything valuable. "It looks like Brad and Abby forgot to look in here."

"No doubt they'd have picked it clean." Caleb hefted the tarp and kicked open the door. She'd have to save the boxes for another time.

Lightning burst in the sky, and thunder cracked as the downpour thickened. Once the shed was bolted, she scurried up the path toward the house, Caleb a mere half step behind. They rounded the corner and hurried toward the tools and lumber in the clearing.

"Go inside. I'll take care of the tarp." Caleb's tone left no room for discussion.

She released the tarp and ran for shelter. Water drizzled through the roof over the porch—a much-needed repair she hadn't noticed until now. She shook out her hair while Caleb secured the sawhorse and lumber. He grabbed his toolbox and cast a quick glance at her before turning toward the parking lot.

"Where are you going?" she called.

Caleb's expression turned as stormy as the weather. "Back to town."

"You can't drive in this. Come in." She motioned for him to join her on the porch, puzzled over his reaction. Was he still shaken up over their earlier hug, or was this part of his usual guarded behavior?

He glanced between her and his truck, then finally jogged toward the house and stepped onto the creaky porch, rivulets of water running from his hairline, down his face and into the neckline of his T-shirt. "I guess you're right. A storm like this could bring a flash flood in the gully."

"Flash flood? It never used to be that bad."

"It's been a long time since the road's been maintained consistently." Caleb's shoulder brushed hers as they watched the rain, and he didn't pull away until her phone rang.

"It's my mom. I need to take this." She held up her finger as she slipped inside the front door, leaving it open a crack. "Haven't heard from you in a few days. How have you been?"

"I was hoping you'd be home by now."

"It's taking longer than I thought. I'd have called, but I thought you were still upset with me for being here."

Robyn roamed from room to room, hunting for anything that could be used to dry off. Nothing. She sat on the plastic lawn chair in the bedroom. "I hope you can understand why I have to do this."

Despite the bad connection, a loud sigh resonated over the line. "You don't know what you're getting yourself into. I wish you'd come home."

Where was Mom's home this week? As long as she could remember, home was entirely dependent on who her mother was dating, and Robyn had promised herself long ago never to live that way.

She nibbled her fingernail. "The property isn't finished yet. It's my responsibility, and I need to make sure everything is taken care of."

"I still don't think it's a good idea, but it sounds like you've made up your mind." Frustration laced Mom's voice. "It's not like I've ever told you what to do, but this time I think you should listen. You know how vicious Brad— and, what's that little one's name? Angie? You know how awful they can be."

"It's Abby, and she's not like she used to be." She was worse, but at least Robyn had hope for a relationship. She stood and paced. "This is what I need to do for closure. Please, try to understand."

"Don't say I didn't warn you."

"What's the worst thing that could happen? Brad and Abby already moved most of the stuff out, and I probably won't see them until the hearing." She peered out the window, pulling away quickly when Caleb caught her.

"What hearing?"

"Never mind. Look, you've never been a worrier, Mom. Don't start now."

"How about this? I won't worry, as long as you don't get your hopes up. Deal?"

Hopes up for what? The property was already legally hers. And any other hopes—like hoping her dad would love and pay attention to her—were already crushed. At least he'd remembered her in the end, and that had to mean something. Right?

"Deal. Trust me. My expectations were low to start with." Abysmally low.

Of course, if she were completely honest, she did hope Caleb felt the chemistry stirring between them, and she hoped to get to know him better. But mostly she hoped to find out why he remained guarded and what secrets he held so close.

What was he doing here? He knew he should've left when he had the chance, but the moment she invited him inside, he caved. The gully was probably still passable, but if he waited much longer he'd be trapped—and he could count off all the reasons why he shouldn't be alone with Robyn.

He kicked himself for hugging her earlier. As if the situation wasn't already tenuous enough. He hoped she didn't see right through him, to the feelings that ignited a fire he'd never experienced before. Thankfully, he'd pulled back before he dove headlong into a kiss. Logic had won out. But it wouldn't continue to do so if he hung around admiring her sun-bleached hair and the way she swung a hammer while she pretended to know what she was doing. Her nice figure and good nature were a lethal combination.

If he didn't tell her the truth now, he'd explode.

Caleb glanced at the trail his shoes left on the hardwood floor. He had to get out of here. He didn't need more complications. The only thing he'd wanted from the start was to do right by Dan. There wasn't supposed to be a beautiful woman on the property to add another layer to sort through.

How long had it been since he'd met a woman so easy to talk to, someone who put him at ease and whose playful tone almost reminded him of the interaction between his own parents? He wanted to know what made Robyn tick and what made her a dutiful daughter after what was obviously a less than ideal childhood. Maybe the attraction existed because she was completely unavailable. Or maybe he was simply having a reaction to all the changes in his life. In his line of work, he'd seen people make crazy decisions under duress. And he was definitely under duress.

One thing was certain, he couldn't go on trying to douse a growing inferno with a garden hose. To snuff out feelings toward the one woman on earth he had no right to be anywhere near. He'd seen the way she wanted to breathe fire on the person responsible for her dad's death, and he couldn't say he didn't blame her. Sometimes it was even hard for him to remember Aaron was the one truly at fault.

Caleb looked out the window for a slice of blue sky as he mulled his options. Not one of them sounded good— or more important, right. As soon as Robyn was off the phone, he could say his piece.

She glanced at the phone in her hand and shook her head with a long, slow sigh. "It was my mom. She's not happy I'm here, but I can't deal with that right now. I'm already on emotional overload. I can't deal with anything else."

A cramp seized his gut. Would there ever be a right time to talk?

"I'd offer you a towel to dry off, but there aren't any. Looks like they took almost everything." Robyn motioned to the sparse front room, where the only piece of furniture was a couch that had seen better days.

Caleb swallowed hard. "I have to go."

"But the storm—"

"Has subsided. For now." He ran his hands down his face, his whiskers sounding like sandpaper.

"Are you sure?" Robyn's nose scrunched. "I feel bad sending you out in this. I'd offer you something to drink, but…" She grimaced.

"Better make sure to get your groceries before the next storm hits." He'd noticed how she picked up only enough food to get by for a day or two. She was probably trying to make her money stretch, but he didn't want to embarrass her by asking the details.

"I'll make a trip tomorrow. Maybe we could go together and hit the hardware store, too. There are a few more things we need."

"About tomorrow—" He paused to gather up a bit of courage, which wasn't easy, considering the hopeful smile teasing Robyn's lips. He couldn't work here at Lakeside with the weight of truth pinning his conscience, yet he'd been so busy he hadn't found a replacement—especially one who would protect her from Brad.

"I'll need your help pricing everything out. I don't have much in the way of savings, and there's so much that needs to be done. Phil mentioned there were some kind of provisions for the repairs, but he didn't get specific—"

"I can't."

"Can't what?" Robyn's feathery eyebrows drew tight.

"Can't do this."

A painful pause stretched between them. Only the sound of rain against the windowpanes offset their silence.

Robyn rolled her lip. "Now you have me worried. Are you upset about what happened earlier?"

"It's nothing like that." He swiped the rain—or maybe it was sweat—from his forehead with the sleeve of his T-shirt. *Tell her.* He turned away and focused his gaze outside, but the only thing he could really see was Dan at the side of the road, asking for help moments before he breathed his last breath. It'd been too late to save him. Even as a crowd formed and Aaron Dirkson sped away, Caleb knew so many lives had been ruined. And he could've stopped it, if he'd only made the right decision. Adrenaline pounded through his veins as memories assaulted him. He drew a fist, not daring to turn and face Robyn. "I'm sorry." His throat tightened so he could barely speak. Barely breathe. "You have no idea how sorry I am, but we've got to talk."

"I'm not sure I'm up to hearing whatever it is." Uncertainty etched across her face. She flicked a glance out the window. "Ginger's back."

A familiar-looking woman climbed out of a red SUV and popped open an umbrella. Her ankles wobbled as she picked her way across the soggy lot on low heels.

Caleb squeezed his eyes, forcing himself not to disintegrate. Standing in the same room without full disclosure was no longer an option. "When I come back, we have to talk." He swiped his hat out of his back pocket and pulled it low over his eyes, then left without saying goodbye. Without making excuses.

Without looking back.

Chapter Nine

Robyn watched Caleb peel out, mud spraying behind his wheels. What on earth would make him react that way? She combed through their conversation for anything that would've caused him to apologize profusely before practically running out the door.

She stepped onto the porch and leaned against the railing, taking in the fresh scent of rain, calling to mind happier times—happier times meaning before Abby figured out that Robyn was more than just some kid that came to play for a few weeks every summer. Once Abby realized Robyn was a daughter just like she was, a battle for their father's attention ensued.

"What was that all about?" Ginger stepped onto the porch.

"I'm not sure." A sick feeling pooled in her stomach. Trying to guess what Caleb wanted to discuss wouldn't do any good. She'd have to deal with it later. For now, she'd be happy the rain was petering out and her friend was here to visit.

"I tried calling. You really should check your messages."

Robyn pulled out her phone. "I don't see anything. The

reception out here is spotty. What brings you by? Must be important to get you out in this weather."

"I just got back to town and I wanted to see you. Plus I thought I'd take some pictures for the website. It sure has changed. You two work fast." Ginger snapped her umbrella shut. "Was that who I saw tearing out of here?"

"It was. I hope he's all right." Robyn stepped off the porch, the earth soft beneath her feet. The rain slowed to a drizzle. "Looks like your timing is perfect. Where would you like to start?"

"Let's walk through the cabins and outbuildings first, and then we can share the bear claws I brought from The Tasty Pastry." Ginger patted her bag. She pulled out her camera and snapped the first shot. "Boy, does this bring back memories. At this angle, the pictures should look good on the website."

"Isn't it a little early for that?"

"I'm just starting to put everything together. No rush." Ginger tucked the camera in the side pocket of her leather purse.

Robyn led the way to the back bedroom and made a mental note to buy a doorknob. "You're right about the memories. I wish that last fight with my dad hadn't happened." She'd allowed too much time to pass without calling him to at least try to right their relationship. Sure, the phone line cut both ways, but she'd been the one to instigate the last argument accusing him of favoritism.

"You have to stop beating yourself up. He's with the Lord now."

"But how do you know? He wasn't a Christian when I knew him."

"You need to talk to Pastor Steve. He probably knew your dad better than anyone else. I'll introduce you next time you come to town." Ginger squeezed Robyn's shoulders in a side hug. "Now, let's see what else Lakeside has to offer."

The women walked the property, alternately taking pictures and reliving childhood memories. Ginger pointed out the buildings still needed attention but the land itself was valuable. The sale would bring in enough to cover the remaining debts with some to spare if everything went as planned. Only now Robyn wasn't as certain as she was before. Though she knew it wasn't possible for her to handle the expense of such a property, the thought tugged at her endlessly.

"That's about it, except for the main house." She closed the door of the boathouse without having a good look beyond all the equipment that would need to be hauled off. She smiled as she remembered Caleb helping her into the canoe and the intensity of his gaze every time they were together. What could he possibly have to say that was so distressing?

"I'd prefer to wait until you get some paint on the new rails of the porch before I take a picture of the main house. And before I forget, here's my friend's card for when you're ready to get an appraisal." Ginger pawed through her bag.

"Wait, what about the storage shed?"

"Trust me, no one wants to see a picture of a shed." Ginger tucked her camera away.

"Let's go down there, anyways. I saw a few boxes I want to bring up to the house." She motioned for Ginger to follow before remembering her friend's leather shoes, already caked with mud.

"You owe me for this." Ginger winked.

The path was slicker than before, and it took both women supporting one another to make it down the hill. Robyn slid open the dead bolt and stepped inside. The boxes might be just what she was looking for, though she wasn't entirely certain what that was. She tried not to get her hopes up since there was probably nothing important inside.

Ginger inched inside and bandied away cobwebs that hung over the doorway. "This better be worth the trip."

"We'll see." She ripped the partially peeling tape off the top of the first box. Files. Was this what Brad had been after?

Ginger peeked over her shoulder. "You dragged me down here for this?"

"It might be important. Let's just take the first two. I'll get the other ones later." She glanced outside as rain started to peck against the tin roof.

"I heard the storm's going to continue into the night and all day tomorrow." Ginger rolled her eyes as though seeking a reprieve from the weather.

"We'll never get to the painting if it keeps up. Let's hurry and get these into the house." She held the box with one arm and maneuvered around the camping equipment. They muddled up the hill, halfway supporting one another and laughing as they made their way toward the main house. She propped the side door open with her foot. "Now where are the bear claws you promised?"

"Patience. Let's see what we've got." Ginger set down her purse and pointed to the box in Robyn's arms. "What's inside that one?"

She yanked the tape off and lifted the flaps. "A photo album!" She lifted it out of the box and cradled it, inhaling the scent of old pages and memories. She sat on the floor and began to leaf through the book. "Well, there's one picture of me," she whispered.

Ginger pulled up a lawn chair. "I told you Dan never forgot about you. Honestly, think about who he married—one picture was probably all she'd allow."

She quieted, realizing her friend was right. All things considered, Robyn was thankful to find at least one keepsake among her dad's belongings.

The engine of a vehicle cut through the patter of rain. Robyn hopped up, her heart filled with the dreaded hope she'd promised her mother she wouldn't feel. "I wonder if Caleb came back."

A flatbed truck.

When she saw who it was, her pulse skipped into double time. She stepped onto the porch and prayed for God to give her an opportunity. Maybe this time things would go better, though the adrenaline slamming through her veins said otherwise.

She went outside, forced a smile and waved hello to Brad and Abby.

Caleb kicked himself for the way he'd left Robyn. He never let his emotions override his logic. It went against his orderly life, but lately the smallest incidents wiped out his good judgment. Not that trying to tell Robyn who he was with her friend standing next to her would've been a show of good judgment.

After stopping at the grocery store for a few essentials, Caleb headed for Phil's office to turn in the extra set of keys to Lakeside Cabins. He knew he was operating out of confusion, but what else could he do?

Phil cast a nonchalant glance at the doorway. "You really need to learn to knock. I could've been with a client."

"And I'm making mistakes left and right."

"Hold that thought." Phil positioned his golf club carefully before putting the ball into the cup. "Aren't you being overly dramatic? That's not like you."

"You're right. I have to get a grip." Caleb sent the keys skittering across the desk. "But maybe that means letting it go. No matter what I do, it's not turning out the way I thought it would. I was trying to help, not hurt." He strode to the window and rested his palms on the sill. "Restoring Dan's place was supposed to be simple. A way to keep my promise to a dying man, and clear my head."

"Let's be honest—you just wanted a way to clear your guilt, not your head."

Caleb wheeled around to face his friend. "You have no right to judge my motives. Is there something wrong with doing right by Dan?" He regretted his sharp tone and instantly held himself in check.

"Nothing wrong with wanting to help, but maybe you're not admitting the real reason." Phil rose and met Caleb's eye. "No matter how hard you work, you can't bring him back."

He turned away, transfixed by the rain battering the window. Conflicting thoughts and emotions pummeled him. "I dishonored the badge. The one thing I told my dad I'd never do. I promised."

The wooden floor groaned under Phil's steps. He gripped Caleb's shoulder and spoke with slow, measured words. "You did not dishonor the badge."

"Then why—" he worked against the tightness in his throat "—why do they have to have a hearing?"

"Procedure. Nothing more."

He nodded to acknowledge he understood, though it did nothing to relieve him of the deeper truth. "Police work was the only thing my dad and me had in common. He was so proud when I graduated from the academy and followed in his footsteps. It was kind of his motto—don't dishonor the badge. I can't imagine what he'd be thinking if he knew about all this."

"He'd know you made the best decision you could under the circumstances. That's all any of us can do."

"So what's the right decision now?" Caleb gritted his teeth. "Every time I try to talk to her, something happens. Or maybe it's me. At this point, I'm out of ideas."

"Tell her who you are and how you feel."

"I'll tell her who I am, and after that she won't care how I feel." He paced the office. "The first woman I'm attracted to in years is the one woman I shouldn't be near. None of it makes sense."

"Does it have to? I've met her a few times, and she's beautiful, spirited and easygoing—the complete opposite of you. Maybe that's the attraction."

"Thanks. Good to know what you really think."

"From what I gather, she's also a woman who loves God and wants to live like it—and that *is* just like you."

"You should've seen the way I blew out of there today. I wanted so badly to tell her everything, but Ginger showed up." He hated to admit he'd had a smidgen of relief.

"The Realtor? I heard she was back."

"Is there anything you don't hear?"

Phil paused and looked up, eyes wide. "I forgot—I heard Brad was going out to the cabins this afternoon. I was in the middle of a lunch meeting when I overheard someone talking, and I meant to call you. How'd that go?"

Caleb's gut clenched. "He hadn't shown up by the time I left. What's going on? Don't see anyone out there for days and all of a sudden it's Grand Central." He snatched the keys off the desk.

"What are you doing?"

"I have to get back out there." His nerves vibrated as he considered what he needed to do.

"But there's a monster storm out there. You might as well stay home." Phil rounded the desk and clicked open the weather page on the computer. "They're saying it's going to be a big one."

"I wonder if Brad's already there."

Phil pointed at the screen. "Think—it's not safe to drive in this. You might as well wait until morning."

The gully that ran perpendicular to the Lakeside property really would be full by morning. There had already been a foot of water when he left. Robyn didn't even have food or a car. What if the gully filled like it had last year when Dan was trapped for two days? Caleb had heard the retelling of that story more than once down at the hardware store. Dan ended up having to take a raft down the lake and hike out for help. Would Robyn know what to do?

Lord, are You trying to tell me something? Caleb rubbed his forehead and hoped God was giving him the chance he needed to talk to Robyn. Going back was the right thing to do. Rain slapped against the window, as if to reinforce his decision.

Caleb turned abruptly. "I have to get to her."

"Are you sure about this? Brad can't be that big a threat." Phil's eyebrow peaked. He took off his glasses and rubbed the bridge of his nose.

Lightning lit up the room. Caleb started for the door. "He is. It was dumb for me to leave her out there in the first place. What was I thinking?"

"Sounds like you weren't."

"You're a lot of help."

"I try."

Caleb had to reach Lakeside before Brad bullied Robyn. Before the gully filled all the way and left her stranded. But if the downpour in the town square was any indication, he might already be too late.

Chapter Ten

Caleb tore out of the office, thankful he'd already picked up some groceries. Robyn would need them if she was trapped. Worse, she might be trapped with Brad. The urgency to reach her intensified with every mile. With any luck, Brad had come and gone, and the only thing Caleb had to worry about was getting to her before the road washed out. No, he had infinitely more to worry about than that, but he refused to give in to the fear that crouched in his gut.

More than likely, she'd tell him to leave and never come back. And though he knew what the ramifications would be, it burned. At least he'd have the chance to make sure she was safe and see her one last time.

It took a storm and the threat of danger, but for the first time in weeks he had clarity. A mission. His choices were gone, and doing the right thing had become simple. It really wasn't about Dan anymore. It certainly wasn't about himself. It was doing what was right for Robyn.

Even if someone else was there—and no matter what her mood—he was going to tell her before she heard it in town. He knew with unshakable certainty that because they'd grown closer she'd be devastated to hear it from anyone but him. What mattered in the beginning didn't matter now. Only truth.

Water pooled on the main road, bringing several cars to a standstill, but thankfully fewer people were on the outskirts of town. Giant puddles pockmarked the dirt road that led to Lakeside, and even with the four-wheel drive engaged, anxiety built inside him with each turn.

Lord, help me get there in time. And give me the courage to be truthful.

The truck jounced over deep ruts, splattering mud all over the windshield. Caleb rounded the bend and pulled to a stop. Rainwater rushed through the gully, nearly reaching the top of the bank. He clicked the wipers on high.

If he crossed too quickly, he risked flooding the engine. Too slowly and his tires could get bogged down in the mud that had already begun to soften since he'd left earlier.

Either way, the truck could be swept away in the current.

He had to find a way. He refused to leave a woman stranded in the storm. Considering the condition of the property, it wouldn't be a surprise if the electricity went out, too.

Caleb scanned the bank, searching for the shallowest point to cross. Then he took his foot off the brake and forded the rising water.

Robyn refused to give in to tears because if she did, she'd drown. With grief over her father's death still fresh, she couldn't bear the harsh treatment from her siblings.

Correction—half siblings.

Brad and Abby had come solely to haul away the rest of the furniture. Rather than gathering as a family to support one another, they were still at odds, even with the upcoming hearing. Brad had demanded to know what was in the boxes and promptly taken them despite Robyn's and Ginger's protests. Then the pair had quickly loaded the armoire, couch and a rolltop desk—using Dad's tarp that had covered Caleb's tools—and left to beat the brunt of the storm.

Reluctantly, Ginger left, too, after helping Robyn haul Caleb's larger tools onto the porch and clean off the pool raft for her to sleep on. Ginger had also offered Robyn a place to stay, which she turned down since there was still too much left to do at Lakeside. Despite the afternoon's drama, Robyn smiled, remembering the warmth of Caleb's touch.

She decided there was no use moping around when there was so much to be done. Besides, she had to do something to keep her mind off the rumble of her stomach since she never had a chance to eat the bear claw from The Tasty Pastry.

Without Caleb's direction, she'd have to start with cosmetic fixes, like scrubbing down the bathrooms in the cabins. She didn't need to wait for the rain to let up for that. She grabbed the bucket and cleaning supplies from under the sink and donned an old pair of rubber gloves that she wasn't at all sure would offer any protection. If she hurried, she could finish before sundown.

A knock startled her. Who in their right mind would come out in this weather?

She hurried to the front, yanked off her gloves and glanced out the window. No car in the lot. She opened the door a crack. "Caleb, what happened?"

Water saturated his hair and clothes and leaked off the plastic bags in his hands. "Take this." He thrust the grocery sacks at her and shed his shoes on the porch.

"You're soaked. Come in and warm up." She set the load on the counter, watching Caleb dry off as best as he could before coming inside. Hope hitched in her chest despite her promise to Mom. Besides, her promise not to hope was related to Dad, and she was in no danger of breaking that one. She ushered Caleb inside. "You came back."

He locked into her gaze, his eyes reflecting an emotion she couldn't quite identify. It looked to be equal parts longing and dread.

Quit overreacting. She'd drive herself crazy if she tried to read into every nuance.

Caleb's mouth softened. He started unpacking the sacks, his shoulder brushing hers. "I couldn't leave you here alone without food. There's no telling when the storm's going to let up, and—" his eyes darted around the room "—I was worried about you."

"You were?" Robyn tried to suppress her smile. Was it possible he cared about her as much as she was coming to care about him?

"I heard Brad was on his way out here."

She sighed, deeply. "He and Abby were here, and now they've left."

"I take it things didn't go so well." The concern in his voice melted her.

"No, but I'm confident God has a plan. He brought me here for a reason." Heat rushed to her face. Hopefully Caleb didn't think she was implying anything to do with him, though it was increasingly clear to her that her feelings were real. And strong.

The lines around his mouth tightened as though he wanted to speak but was holding back.

Robyn lifted the grocery sacks. "I don't know what to say. Thank you. You really didn't have to do that." Though her stomach was eternally grateful. There was something endearing about a man who bought three boxes of cereal, crackers and a few cans of soup. She wandered back to the front window before she got too cozy and accidentally revealed too much. "Where's your truck?"

"The engine flooded when I crossed the creek." Caleb peeled off his outer shirt and used it to towel off his hair. The dark tips spiked in a messy, uninhibited way that was wholly opposite from the man she knew.

She caught herself staring and turned away. "Creek? There's not a creek between here and town."

"There is now." Caleb cocked his head.

"I…" Robyn clutched the cross on her necklace, suddenly unable to form a coherent sentence. How would he get home? Would his truck be okay? And why did he think she was important enough to risk coming for? She swallowed her questions and forced a steady tone. "Let's eat."

She opened a can of soup and box of crackers while she allowed reality to sink in. Despite the tragedy of her father's death, the problems with Brad and Abby—not to mention her bank account—a change was taking place in her life. She could feel it every time she was with Caleb and every time she thought about making a life in Pine Hollow. Staying still didn't seem like a possibility, but on some level it felt so right.

"I'm embarrassed to say this, but I have no way to heat up the soup. No pots or pans. But we can eat it out of cups. See?" She held up a mug she'd washed earlier in the day.

"I should have thought of that. Sorry." Caleb leaned against the door frame, hands shoved deep into his pockets. He met her gaze then looked away, his confidence seeming to wane.

"Not a problem—really." She poured the soup into the mugs and handed one to Caleb. "Let's take our picnic into the living room." She grinned, hoping to put him at ease. "Wait here and I'll be right back." She went to the bedroom and retrieved the blanket—the only one in the house—off the makeshift bed. She'd have to figure out something else to use for cover tonight, because she certainly couldn't let him sit and shiver through dinner after all he'd gone through. "Here you are—" she raised her hand as he started to protest "—and I won't take no for an answer."

Caleb shifted, hardly glancing up from his position on the floor, as she draped the worn blanket around his broad shoulders. His hair smelled of fresh rain, and it was all Robyn could do not to linger. She took up her cup and sat cross-legged, closer than she should have.

"What's going to happen with your truck?" She sent up a quick prayer of thanks before taking a large drink of room-temperature soup.

"It should be fine after it dries out." Caleb toasted her with his mug and took a swig. Then he looked away. "I knew better, but there was no other way across."

"I'm flattered you'd do that." She swirled the soup in the mug. *Lord, help.* There was obviously something on his mind, something he wanted to share but couldn't. Maybe once he warmed up he'd be open to conversation. She laid her hand on his forearm and dipped her head to meet his eye. "You have no idea how much I needed the kindness." She drew a sorrowful breath. "It's been a hard afternoon."

Caleb nodded, his eyes taking on a glow as lightning brightened the room. He didn't pull away from her touch, and it took several moments before she realized she still had hold of his arm. Her pulse danced as she retracted her hand.

They ate in silence, both gazing out the window at the flashes of lightning that closed in on Lakeside. She offered him the box of crackers. "The storm doesn't seem to be letting up. It looks like you might be stuck."

"You have no idea." He leaned against the wall and stared at the ceiling.

She chose her words carefully and added a lilt to her voice. "In that case, what do you suppose you'll do?"

Caleb turned to face her, grim lines forming around his mouth. "What I always do—pray."

"Sometimes prayer is the only thing that helps." She examined his expression. Were they still talking about the same thing?

Caleb stood and folded the blanket. He handed it to Robyn, his hand brushing over hers and sending a shock wave that stole her breath. Their gazes locked, and for an instant, she saw a yearning in his eyes that was both powerful and raw. She drew the blanket to herself, reeling him in with it, their faces a mere breath apart.

In a swift motion, he drew back and ran his hands through his hair. "There's another reason I'm here."

"I'm just glad you came back." Maybe she really *didn't* want to know what was on his mind—not if it would drive him away as it had this afternoon.

He walked to the window, arms folded, his back to her. Silence wrapped around her like a vine, choking off whatever feelings she thought she was starting to have. She began to speak, but her resolve drained, leaving her with the same sick sensation she'd had when she first saw Brad and Abby.

"I should've told you the moment you came to Lakeside." His voice was scratchy and low, matching the rumble of thunder outside.

"Whatever it is can't be that bad." She wanted to reach out and comfort him, but conflicting emotions rooted her to the ground, rooted her to reality. She had no doubt that this went far beyond property renovations and stalled trucks.

Caleb turned, his body cast in a dark silhouette. "I have something to say, and you're not going to like it."

Chapter Eleven

Caleb's pulse ratcheted up. Where was all the bravado he'd mustered on the way to Lakeside? What seemed like a good idea moments before now appeared foolish in light of Robyn's blue gaze drilling him. Still, no matter how she responded, it wouldn't be as bad as his self-inflicted flogging. The truth would set him free. Only he didn't want to be free of Robyn, and that's exactly what would happen.

Robyn stepped back, an air of defensiveness around her. "I'm sure there's nothing you could tell me that's any worse than what I've already been through."

Thunder rumbled low, drowning out the blood hammering inside his head. He wiped his palms on his jeans. "It's about your dad."

Robyn clutched her necklace, uncertainty etched on her face. "So you know more than you let on?"

A tide of guilt washed over him. Robyn didn't deserve this. From the start, she'd been open with him, always friendly and kind. Always drawing him into conversation, even when he didn't want to be and causing him to forget the burden he carried. And he was about to blow it all.

He released a frustrated breath. "I told the truth when you asked what he'd said about you—I hadn't known him well enough for him to talk to me about his kids." He raked his hand through his wet hair. His chest seemed to tighten with each moment that brought him closer to the inevitable. "I was there that day."

"You mean—" Robyn covered her mouth, and her face paled "—you saw what happened?"

Not only had he seen it happen in real time but the scene replayed in his head like an endless, horrifying looped video. Aaron Dirkson running the red light. The chase through town. The teen's car heading toward the lone pedestrian. Dan Dawson on the side of the road.

Caleb nodded. "You'd better have a seat."

"No, I'm fine." Robyn's sharp tone softened to a plea, causing sympathy to surge in his chest. "Maybe you can fill in the gaps and tell me the things no one else could. I have to know."

"Aaron Dirkson moved here from Phoenix about a year ago."

"That's the kid. Right?" Robyn's eyes turned watery. She cradled her arms around her middle.

"Yes, and he was trouble from the start. Underage drinking parties, vandalism—things that would go unnoticed in the big city but get you a lot of negative attention in Pine Hollow." He shoved his hands into his pockets to keep from wiping away the lone tear that trailed down Robyn's cheek. He had to keep reminding himself that he had no right to offer comfort. "More than once he was caught ditching school and getting liquored up with a few other boys. Juvie never seemed to have much of an impact on him, and the cycle continued."

"How do you know so much about him?" Robyn twined her fingers, her eyebrows pinched.

"I'll get to that, but let's just say that everyone in town knows about Dirkson."

A strong gust rattled the windowpanes. He glanced outside. This wasn't a conversation he wanted to hurry, but time was critical. He needed to see if his engine had dried out so he could cross the gully. Being trapped at Lakeside under these circumstances was not an option.

"So what happened?" Robyn grazed his arm.

He cleared his throat. "The day of the accident, Dirkson had already been spotted loitering with friends behind the pizza joint during school hours. Because of his record, it was natural to assume he'd been drinking." Which was the only reason Caleb refused to let him go after he ran the red light.

Robyn frowned. "It's my understanding that the kid wasn't under the influence during the accident."

"No one knew that until later." He swallowed, remembering how desperate he was for the reports to come back with a different finding. If only they had, no one would've questioned his judgment in chasing Aaron down. "It was imperative to get Dirkson off the road."

"Thank God he will be for a long time. At least with so many eyewitnesses, there's no mistaking who did it. That kid needs to be locked up." Robyn seemed to release her breath, her shoulders slumping in relief. "I feel bad for Aaron's family. They must be devastated, too."

"I suppose so, but they're a hard family to figure out."

He'd tried to warn the Dirksons, letting them know where Aaron would eventually end up. He'd even gone so far as to give them information—on an unofficial basis—about programs for troubled teens available at the youth center. Too bad no one listened, including the chief, who told Caleb to keep it professional after the Dirksons complained. Even though everyone knew Aaron was the poster child for a troubled teen, when one of the town's most well-known citizens was killed, Caleb still came out the bad guy.

"I appreciate you telling me this, but I've heard it all before. The only part I hadn't heard was about the police officer." She flinched. "When Ginger told me the whole thing could've been prevented, I was shocked. It just seems so careless. Even if they thought the kid had been drinking, making him drive faster seems like such a dumb move. That's why we're all so anxious for the hearing. Dad deserves justice from everyone involved." Robyn glanced skyward, as though trying to shake off the anger. "Anyway, you said you were there. Are you one of the eyewitnesses that came forward?"

"Not exactly." He backed away and paced the room. There was no easy way to give himself up. He had to take the consequences like a man. At the moment, he was more concerned with her reaction than with keeping his badge. *One thing at a time, Sloane.* He stopped in front of Robyn and trapped her with his gaze. His heart jackhammered when he opened his mouth. "I was behind Dirkson…in the police cruiser."

Seconds ticked by. Conflicting emotions skimmed Robyn's face, until finally her eyes narrowed. "I'm confused. What do you mean you were *in* the police car?"

Caleb squared his shoulders, took a breath. Said a prayer. "It was me. I made the call."

Robyn drew back. A bolt of shock ricocheted inside her. She tried to rethink Caleb's words, to make them mean something other than what he said. There was no way the handyman was responsible for chasing Aaron through town until he killed her father. It simply wasn't possible.

Caleb's throat bobbed in a hard swallow. "Please, say something."

A thousand thoughts vied for her attention. She strode to the window and rested against the sill. She shook her head, allowing a smidgen of relief to work its way through the confusion. She smiled. "I think I heard you wrong. You scared me for a second." She clutched her throat, allowing her breath to catch up. "You mean you called in the accident. Right?" She faced Caleb. "I'm sure you did everything you could. It probably happened so fast."

He stood, motionless. "I did call it in, but that's not what I meant." His jaw flexed, and his gaze shot around the room, finally landing on her with such empathy she wanted to cry. "I'm the officer who pursued Dirkson."

"You're a handyman." She squeezed her eyes. This wasn't happening. None of it made sense, and she really didn't need him to complicate her situation any more than it already was.

"I'm a third-generation police officer. I've been with the Pine Hollow Police Department for six years." His gaze never wavered.

"Then what are you doing at Lakeside?" Robyn's voice reached a pitch she hadn't heard since the fight when she walked out on her father—the last time she saw him alive. "Why are you out here swinging a hammer and fixing porches and…" Her hand curled into a ball as she fought against the rage simmering in her chest. "Oh, I get it. You're on leave, am I right? You haven't inflicted enough misery on this family, so you think to yourself, hey, I might as well cash in by fixing up Dan's place while I wait it out." She buried her face in her hands, willing herself not to cry. Or at least not to allow him to see the tears when they came.

The floorboards groaned.

"Don't come near me." She held up her hand. "Just stay away."

Caleb stopped. He remained silent, though she desperately wished he'd say something—anything—to fight back and give her a reason to shout and release her pent-up emotions. Instead, he kept his distance, a distance that allowed her to give in to grief.

"You knew." She folded her arms and looked everywhere but directly at Caleb. "This whole time, you knew, and you said nothing. Why? You've had plenty of opportunities. I feel so foolish." That's what she got for trusting a man she'd just met. And here she'd vowed not to be like her mother, always swayed by the next handsome face.

"You have no reason to feel foolish." Caleb's tone was gentle, soothing.

"I have every reason. I actually thought…" She caught herself before confessing that she believed he was falling for her, the same way she was falling for him. She moved to the door. "Never mind. What I thought isn't important. What matters is that I know who's responsible for the accident. That's all I wanted."

Caleb took a step closer and then seemed to think better of it. "I don't think that's all you wanted."

"What do you mean by that?"

"I think you wanted the situation with your dad to have ended differently." He moved slowly toward the door. Toward her. "I think you wanted to find a way to make yourself feel better about your relationship."

"That's none of your business. I'd never have told you if I'd known who you are." She folded her arms defiantly. How dare he judge her motives? He had no right.

"You believed that seeing the officer fired would make up for the time you missed with your dad. Just like overseeing the sale of the property would make you feel better." Caleb took another slow step, the way one would approach a frightened animal. "You as much as said so."

"And is that why you're here, too—guilt?" She hoped her sharp tone cut the same way his confession had.

"I'm here to keep my promise to your dad. He was so scared. I'll never forget the fear in his voice when he begged me to help him. Moments before he breathed his last, I gave him my word. I promised to do everything in my power to help him, and that's what I'm doing. I want to honor his memory." Uncertainty flickered in his dark eyes, as though unsettled emotions warred behind the tough exterior.

"Honor? If that were true, you'd have told me from the start."

Caleb winced, and he offered a small nod, his facade all but gone. "I'm sorry you got hurt."

"I'm *not* hurt," she said, more for her benefit than his.

"I am."

The whispered words sent a shiver through her. She wanted to believe him so much that it caused a dull ache, a longing she couldn't explain.

Caleb approached, standing between her and the door. His shoulders sloped, and for an instant, he appeared as deeply affected as she. "I know you don't want to hear it, but I promised myself I'd be totally honest when I came back this time. About everything."

"You're right—I don't." She looked everywhere but at Caleb. She didn't dare.

"I just want to say that if circumstances were different, I believe we might have had something between us." A pained silence followed. "At least *I* felt it."

Robyn steeled herself against the torrent of emotions. Even now, she could feel the attraction flow like a current. What kind of daughter was she? She refused to give in to Caleb's slick words. She'd seen manipulative men before, men who used their good looks and said just the right things to get their way. She was not going there, and nothing he could say would change her mind.

Sure, Caleb had finally outed himself, but in Pine Hollow it was only a matter of time before she'd found out, anyway. Did he really think he was being noble? Then to admit that he might have had feelings for her was about as low as a man could sink.

Robyn shook her head, disgusted. "You have a lot of nerve. You're probably only saying that because you don't want me to lobby against you to the review board. I doubt there's a sincere bone in your body."

"You've got it wrong."

"Not this time. In fact, it's probably the first time I've gotten it right." She reached around him for the doorknob, bracing herself to watch him go. "It's time for you to leave."

Caleb paused in the doorway. "For what it's worth, I'm sorry. More than you'll ever know. I pray someday you can forgive me."

Sorry would never begin to cover her loss. She locked the door behind him, thankful he was gone, because when it all came down to it, there was no difference between Caleb and the men she'd seen come and go out of her mother's life.

No difference, whatsoever.

Chapter Twelve

Sunlight pierced Caleb's eyes. He lifted his arm to block it, but with the seat-belt buckle poking his ribs, he was done sleeping. It'd been years since he'd slept in his truck. In fact, the last time was when his dad kicked him out after he'd skipped a week of school in favor of midday parties at an abandoned farm. He could've easily been an Aaron Dirkson, and he tried never to forget it. Then why was it so hard to forgive the kid?

He grabbed the steering wheel and pulled himself upright. One glance at the gully behind him caused him to groan. Though the stream had slowed to little more than a trickle, the muddy banks made the road impassable.

He turned the key in the ignition. The engine coughed but refused to come to life. Great. Stuck in the middle of the forest with nowhere to go but back to the woman who'd made him leave.

The pain on Robyn's face had made him sick. The way she'd tried to convince herself he wasn't who he said he was only confirmed what he already suspected: she had feelings for him, too. Feelings that went beyond the simple courtesy that two people had when they worked together.

And, unfortunately for him, feelings that would no longer be mutual.

He climbed out of the truck and powered up his phone, hoping to get ahold of Pastor Steve, who had a tow kit on his pickup. The no-signal icon crushed that idea. There was no other choice but to head back to Lakeside and pray he'd find his way out of the dead zone.

The smell of fresh, wet pine permeated the air, and birds flitted between the trees, as though taking advantage of the lull between back-to-back storms. He held his phone aloft as he trudged through the mud, his socks still wet from walking to the truck after the fiasco with Robyn. He wondered how she was feeling today and if she was settled enough with the news to possibly talk, though he suspected forgiveness was out of the question.

The road narrowed before curving around and opening to the meadow. With the cabins in sight, he stopped and checked his phone. Finally, a signal. He found Pastor Steve's number.

"You're getting a mighty early start!" Pastor Steve's voice resembled a foghorn.

Caleb cringed. He hadn't considered how early it was. "Sorry. Do you think you can come pull out my truck? It died on the road to Lakeside Cabins. I'm stuck. The engine cut out when I crossed the gully." With one eye on the main house, he paced the lot. Was Robyn awake? She was probably eating the cereal he'd brought while he waited outside, stomach rumbling. He rested against the Lakeside Cabins sign, now tarnished and missing the *L* and both *S*'s. It shouldn't be too hard to pull the sign out of the ground and scrap it—only it was no longer his job.

"Is there even a road out there anymore? Is it passable, or am I going to get stuck, too? You might need to get a real tow truck." Pastor Steve yawned over the line. "Listen, I have a meeting with someone in less than an hour. But how about I give you a call when I'm done, and we can decide what to do?"

Caleb rubbed the scruff on his cheek. Pastor Steve was right—asking someone to pull him out *wasn't* reasonable, at least until the mud hardened into something resembling a road. It was at least a six-mile hike back to the main turn-off, but maybe someone could pick him up there. "How about I call you later after I check out the road?"

"Sounds like a plan. We'll have to pray the storm doesn't strike again. We'll figure something out. By the way," Pastor Steve said, issuing a nervous chuckle, "word has it Chief is busy pulling up all your records."

"I expected he would. I can't even get him to call me back." Caleb slapped his fist against the sign. He knew the chief would dig up old dirt—that was to be expected—but more strikes against him would ensure his swift exit from the force. Not that his record hadn't been exemplary, but a few missteps in his early days wouldn't help his cause. "What else have you heard?"

"The review board members have their lips zipped. I know that's policy, but the thing that bugs me is that they stopped looking me in the eye. Every last one of them," Pastor Steve mumbled, as though apologizing for the faceless members of the board. "Just thought you should know."

"Thanks for the heads-up. I'll call you later." He disconnected. Frustration lapped over him in waves. His father's words thundered in his head. *Don't dishonor the badge.* The only accomplishment that earned his father's approval was doing the uniform proud. And one critical mistake would take it all away. For the first time since his dad's death, Caleb was glad his father wasn't around to see it happen.

He dialed Phil, hoping for a ride at the main highway

but got sent straight to voice mail. He left a message and hung up.

"What are you doing back here?" Robyn's voice scattered the birds.

Caleb snapped out of his thoughts. He hadn't even heard her come outside. Words eluded him. He scratched his morning whiskers, suddenly desperate for a shower and a breath mint. He gestured over his shoulder. "My truck is still stuck down by the gully."

Robyn fisted her hands on her tiny waist, seemingly unaware she couldn't possibly look threatening in a smiley face T-shirt and pajama bottoms imprinted with tropical fish. "You mean to tell me you're going to be here even longer?"

He was half hoping she'd be concerned that he'd slept outside, but her comment only confirmed that she had no room for forgiveness. Somehow he had to smooth things over until someone could drive out to get him. Even walking the short distance from his truck had been miserable with wet socks and squishy shoes.

"I'll make you a deal," Caleb said in his most placating tone.

She folded her arms and held a stance that proclaimed she was both annoyed and thoroughly unimpressed.

He scrounged enough courage to continue. "While I wait to get a tow, I'll start working on the roof."

Robyn's eyebrow hitched. "For free?"

Why would she assume otherwise? He was puzzled for a moment until he realized she never knew he was not only working for free but also footing the entire bill. But if he said so now, she'd think he was trying to earn his way back on her good side for all the wrong reasons.

"Of course. And I'll be gone as soon as I can get a tow truck or a ride at the turnoff."

Her eyes darted to the floorboards beneath her bare feet. Her mouth tightened as though she couldn't decide whether it was worse to risk the porch roof falling on her head or to have him around another day.

"Look, you still need the help, and I won't bother you. If I had another way out, I'd leave. Believe me, I tried last night before I gave up and crashed out in my truck." He wasn't above fishing for sympathy.

Robyn's shoulders drooped. "Fine. But please leave me alone." Her voice nearly disappeared in the breeze. She went inside and closed the door with a soft click.

He glanced at the pile of wet lumber. Where was the tarp? And his tools? In all the chaos last night, he hadn't noticed them missing. Finally he spotted the sawhorse and his larger tools next to the porch swing. He couldn't guess why, and he didn't dare ask Robyn.

With a prayer on his lips, he hunted around for the shingles he'd set aside last night, wishing he'd thought to bring his toolbox from his truck. Soon, his prayer turned into whistling a song they sang at church. Out of everything, he missed worship time the most. He wanted to go back, but surviving an entire service would be an ordeal with all Dan's friends in attendance.

The weight of his circumstances pressed heavily against his conscience the more he thought about the people in town. How was it that so few stood by his side, even after all the work he'd done outside of his job, like scrounging up a grant to start the youth center and helping with the homeless? He understood the shared grief over losing Dan, but many seemed to want to blame him as much as Aaron.

He stopped working, his spirit suddenly deflated. He'd been desperate to avoid the obvious dilemma that the more he prayed, the worse things got. *Lord, show me where You are in this. Where have I gone wrong? I need help.*

I need hope. He refocused on his work, not entirely sure God heard him.

Suddenly the front door flew open, and a seemingly disembodied arm dropped a plastic bag onto the welcome mat before withdrawing. He set aside the shingles he was hauling, then climbed the steps, wary of what he might find. He peered inside the grocery sack.

Cereal and a mug.

Well, at least he had that.

Robyn leaned her head against the door and whispered a jumbled, inarticulate prayer. She could no longer decipher what she needed or even wanted out of the situation but clung to the hope that God knew. Just when she thought she had her scattered emotions in check, Caleb showed up. Only this time instead of her heart rolling on high tide every time he glanced her way, she wanted to tell him off.

But rather than venting her anger, she'd given him food. She hoped he didn't take it wrong, but even more than that she hoped he'd stop whistling because now she had a worship song in her head when she'd rather be angry.

Lord, what are You doing? Now I have to forgive him, too. I'm just not ready.

She went back to her spot on the floor and closed her Bible. After her morning prayers, she'd paged through her favorite scriptures, hoping to find a passage that would wrap her in peace. Instead, the same unsettled feeling stirred inside her, keeping her cautious and alert and desperately wishing for a place to call home. For a family who cared. The assurance of her father's love.

Last night she'd called her mom after Caleb left, and she'd toyed with the idea of walking away and leaving the whole ugly mess behind. Mom had told her, once again, that she was opening a can of worms by being there, then proceeded to say she'd broken up with her latest boyfriend. No wonder she wanted Robyn to come back.

She peeked out the window and watched Caleb carrying piles of shingles from behind one of the cabins. Powerful muscles worked beneath his T-shirt, muscles she'd assumed came from construction jobs. She'd never have pictured him wearing a badge and toting a gun.

She decided to give cleaning another try, after her previously abandoned effort. She took the bucket and gloves and went out the side door toward cabin one to give it a thorough and long overdue scouring. She stopped around the side of the building to turn on the water.

The musty smell inside reminded her how much she still had to fix before she could list Lakeside. What was she going to do without Caleb? She had to think of something right away or risk spending more time in Pine Hollow. Funny, she wasn't nearly as drawn to the town as she had been before Caleb's revelation.

The toilet gurgled as the tank filled. She quickly set to work, noxious fumes making her wish she had natural cleaners to work with. Unfortunately, the window refused to budge and the vapors grew stronger, even as she stooped over and started on the tub.

The sound of water hitting tile made her stop scrubbing and turn around. She groaned. Water drizzled from the bottom of the tank. She hopped up and ran outside, the screen door slamming behind her. Quickly, she turned off the water.

"What happened? Is everything okay?" Caleb called across the clearing.

"There's a leak in the bathroom. It's one problem after another around here. I can't believe Dad let everything go." She hated the desperate quality in her voice. Worse, she hated that she spoke to Caleb before remembering her anger.

"Let's have a look at it." Caleb turned the water back on and headed inside.

"Why'd you do that?" She scurried after him. "I told you there's a leak."

"We'll turn it off in here." He glanced over his shoulder with a confidence that left her without another word of protest. Maybe she should have thought of that, but she didn't want to admit as much. He turned the water off at the spigot and peered underneath. "I'll have to grab my wrench."

"I saw one in the house."

"Good. Mine's back at the truck." Caleb looked up at her, matter-of-factly. Surely he wasn't trying to get sympathy for having spent the night outside, because no way did he deserve it.

She hurried out of the cabin and darted across the lot, mentally kicking herself for allowing him to step in. Why was he being so helpful? Did he think his kindness would dissuade her from going in front of the committee? He couldn't be more wrong. Quickly, she returned with the wrench, eager for him to finish.

"Thanks. I wasn't quite ready to hike out to the gully and back." Caleb grabbed the wrench and situated himself on the floor. He smelled of sawdust and a long night, and no matter how she struggled against it, sympathy tugged on her heart.

"The sooner we get this over with, the better." The harsh words felt foreign on her lips.

"Thanks for breakfast." Caleb worked the wrench a few times then sat up.

"Just returning the favor."

He nodded, then turned the water back on and waited

for the tank to refill. The leak flowed freely, and water splattered against the warped floorboards.

Robyn pointed. "I think you turned it the wrong way. It's righty-tighty."

"I'll keep that in mind." He turned the water off and resumed his position on the floor, dodging the water, which dripped until the tank was empty again.

She refused to let Caleb's kindness sway her since there was only one reason he was being nice. No doubt that was his plan all along: win her over and shut her up. She scrutinized him, her heart firmly set. "You're doing lefty-loosey again. My right—you're upside down."

"I don't think— Never mind." Caleb finished tightening the bolt. He sat up and turned on the water. Still broken. He turned the knob and stood. "I'll have to get to the hardware store and pick up…" He stopped short of finishing his thought. "Whoever takes over the job will have to pick up some parts to get this fixed."

"I'll be sure to let them know." She stood as far back from Caleb as possible in the tiny space. "So what happens now? Does the chief have the final say about your job, or the review board?" She ignored the erratic rhythm of her heart.

"Why do you want to know? Whatever you have to say can be said to me. Right here, right now."

Heat singed her cheeks. How dare he chastise her! "Trust me, you don't want to know what I really think."

Caleb's eyes darkened. He set the wrench on the counter with a clatter then stormed out. The door slammed behind him, and the cabin felt painfully empty.

Tears bit her eyes, but she adamantly refused to give in to the overwhelming emotions.

How was it possible to be more confused and uncertain than before?

Chapter Thirteen

Robyn worked diligently to scrub out the cabins, as well as the small voice inside that urged her to apologize. Why should she? Caleb was responsible for the death of her dad and, consequently, the death of her chance to make amends. She *would* have done so one day, when the opportunity was right. Now all she was left with was the off chance that she could forge a relationship with Abby—only Abby, since reuniting with Brad seemed out of the question.

She tossed the gloves into the bucket and turned off the water in the kitchen. Cabin four, the largest of the bunch, had always taken the longest to clean. Whenever she and Ginger had finished, they usually extracted their pay in fudge pops. She could practically taste the cool chocolaty goodness, and it made her want to get to town to see her friend. She'd tried calling, but there was no service on her cell. And now she was stuck with Caleb.

Caleb.

Even his name drew her shoulders into knots. For him to be hammering away like he still belonged, he must be crazy. What other reason would he have for continuing to work after their argument? Didn't he see how pointless it was and that no matter how many shingles he nailed she'd still go to the review board? It only made sense that she'd seek justice.

She exited the cabin and locked the door, then hurried across the clearing to avoid Caleb. She also wanted to avoid the hunch that he was as desperate for peace as she was. Finding common ground with him was dangerous, and she refused to go there.

The sound of a nail gun punctured the quiet. She stopped at the side of the main house and snuck a glance at Caleb. He'd skipped lunch, and judging by how low the sun hung in the sky, it was past dinnertime. He was probably hungry, but she didn't dare offer him another meal, no matter how bad she felt for him.

Caleb set the nail gun aside and stretched. Then he stood on the roof and tested his work. Robyn caught herself staring and quickly looked away. He must've contacted the slowest-moving tow truck in Pine Hollow, and she could only pray it got there before another storm hit. There was no way she could force him to sleep in his truck again, rather than offer him one of the cabins—she simply didn't have it in her. But doing so would send the wrong message.

She glanced at the darkening sky. Rain drizzled like a faucet ready to turn up the pressure. She hoped she didn't lose the electricity like she had last night. Sitting in the dark was no fun. Sitting in the dark after learning exactly who she'd unwittingly set her sights on was pure torture.

No, if she was going to be miserable, she'd rather it be with light.

Decision made, she put away the cleaning supplies, donned an old rain slicker she'd found at the back of a closet and headed out back. She remembered seeing camping equipment inside the shed. A lantern or flashlight would help get her through the long night while she leafed through her Bible for comfort.

Mud kicked up with each step, and the soles of her flip-flops refused to grip the ground. She held out her arms for balance, wobbling down the slope, over the rocks and weeds, toward the shed. The door opened with a groan. The room was dank and seemed to have several more cobwebs than when she'd come in here with Ginger.

She picked through the first few items, wary of creepy crawlies that had more than likely taken up residence over the years. An exhaustive search produced three candles and a flashlight without batteries. Dad obviously hadn't planned on going camping anytime soon.

She caught herself midthought. What *had* his last plans been? Had he wanted to get out of Pine Hollow, or had he been content to spend his days at Lakeside, sitting at the dock with a fishing pole? Had he ever considered reaching out to her?

With the candles bundled under her rain slicker, she closed the shed and started up the narrow path. Her toe caught a rock, and her arms windmilled as she braced herself for the fall. Pain rocketed through her ankle and all the way up her left leg.

She pulled in a large breath and winced as she shifted on the cold, wet ground to right herself. Mud covered her hands and legs, making it impossible to check for blood. Gingerly, she fingered her rapidly swelling ankle. The house was still a good thirty yards away, and she hadn't yet navigated the steepest part of the slope. She wondered why her dad had to put the shed so far away.

Robyn pushed against the ground and attempted to stand with all her weight on one leg. The slick mud sucked her back down, but she tried again. Gently applying pressure on her left foot, she tried to take a step uphill, nearly landing her where she started. She ground her teeth, determined to make it work since she couldn't very well spend the night outside.

Like Caleb.

She winced, this time from a pain in her heart. Going soft was not an option.

"What happened? Are you okay?" Caleb appeared near the house and broke into a jog.

The only thing worse than falling was having someone know about it, especially if that someone was Caleb. She steadied herself and pretended the pain was minimal. "I took a little spill."

Caleb skittered down the slope. "Little?" His tone was light, almost teasing, but she knew better than to read too much into it. At this point, she couldn't afford to let him get to her. From now on, she would have to be the one with the tough exterior, speaking only when necessary, like he had when they first met. Now it all made sense.

She forced herself forward, mortified at the pronounced hobble. She looked heavenward for relief. "Really, I'm fine."

"Let me help you back to the house." Beads of rain dripped from his hair. He stood firm, blocking the path.

"I can make it. Just because I'm covered in mud and look like—"

"Your looks aren't the problem." A flash of red washed over his face, and he quickly backpedaled. "What I meant was that I saw you limp. You need help."

She attempted another step. The pain shut down any thoughts of going it alone. She didn't imagine Caleb would allow her to crawl up the hill through the mud, no matter how awkward their relationship. No—it wasn't a relationship. Whatever secret hopes she'd harbored would never be realized.

"But your shirt, it's white." She bit her lip, half of her

hoping he'd realize what he was offering and back out, the other half of her wondering how it'd feel to nestle inside his arms.

"It's just a shirt." Caleb swallowed, his eyes fixed on her with a fierce intensity. "We have more important issues to deal with."

Like she needed the reminder.

With a nod, she relented. Caleb hesitated before placing his arm around her torso for support. She leaned into him, the faint scent of sawdust reminding her how diligently he'd worked all day despite their differences. He tugged her forward, taking the slope in baby steps.

"That's it," he coaxed, his voice smooth enough to lull her into feeling comfortable and safe. "We're almost there. I never could figure why that shed is so far from the house."

"I guess there's a lot about my dad and his thinking I haven't figured out." Robyn stopped and used him to prop herself up while she swiped a strand of wet hair off her face.

Caleb tightened his grip, and it was the first time she remembered feeling such strength and comfort from a man. Even her dad had been a reluctant hugger and only did so when the occasion specifically called for it. Her body warmed at Caleb's touch, and even the patter of rain against the surrounding foliage faded. She could feel him draw each breath, and for the moment they melded together. She found herself almost wishing the walk to the house wouldn't end—and hating that she felt that way.

"I think we're going to make it." The smile in Caleb's voice infused her with a cautious feeling of expectation, as though for a brief moment it didn't matter who they were and what kept them apart.

She dared to look up and catch his gaze. "I hope so."

Caleb's dark eyes rang with emotions clear enough to

read: longing, trepidation, sorrow. She searched his face, the tilt of his mouth and the flex of his jaw, the hard swallow as though he were holding back from saying or doing something regrettable. Or was it all in her imagination?

"Let's get you inside." He opened the door and helped her through. They tottered to the front room, and he tugged off her rain slicker. "What were you doing out back? It's getting dark and I don't have to tell you it's dangerous."

She reached for the candles inside the slicker. "I wanted to make sure I had light tonight. I think I saw matches in the drawer by the stove."

Caleb disappeared into the kitchen, giving her a moment of reprieve from the emotions surging inside her. Whatever relationship she'd hoped might develop just couldn't. He'd misrepresented himself, allowing her to believe he was a local handyman with no ulterior motive. And she was loath to remember why, exactly, he'd done that. She willed herself to shake off the momentary distraction caused by his kindness. Helping her up the hill was what any decent man would've done.

And she knew Caleb was anything but decent.

She heard him rummage through the drawer before returning. "Found them." He reached for the candles, grazing her hands. "Let me take care of those."

The match hissed, and the smell of sulfur filled the space between them. He lit each candle and set them on a chipped plate to catch the wax. The candlelight flickered, illuminating his face against the shadows of the darkening room. Caleb's gaze seared her.

Heat climbed into her cheeks. She lowered her eyes and focused on the mud stain on his shirt. "Thank you. I'm glad you were here to help."

"Me, too." The simple words sent a shiver down her arms. He grabbed the blanket from the floor where she had curled up earlier and draped it over her. "You need to warm up. You're trembling."

Unfortunately, her trembling had nothing to do with the temperature, and it upset her to realize it. She had to stay on guard.

At that moment, caught between anger and forgiveness, repulsion and desire, Robyn made up her mind. She had to get Caleb off the property as soon as possible, because she simply couldn't trust herself to completely shut out the man responsible for her father's death.

The candlelight accented the uncertainty in Robyn's eyes. Hadn't he said and done all the right things? And still she seemed wary. He'd been looking for Robyn to tell her the section of roof covering the porch was finished when he discovered her on the back side of the house, in the mud. Natural instinct took over before he had a chance to remember how hurt he was after the way she'd gone for his jugular.

Still, he knew that grief changed otherwise affable people into irrational, emotional wrecks. Not that Robyn's behavior was irrational, necessarily, but he sure wouldn't mind if she would find it in her heart to forgive him.

"Would you like me to fix you something to eat?" He glanced at the kitchen, wondering if she was sick of cereal and soup, which was the mainstay of his diet lately.

"I don't…" Robyn licked her lips, and her eyebrows drew together. "That'd be nice. I think there's chicken soup left. And help yourself to whatever's there."

He offered a tentative smile before he strode to the kitchen, allowing a glimmer of hope to seep into his heart. He opened a can of soup and poured two cups and then returned to the living room. "Here we are." He handed her one of the mugs. "Room temperature, just like you like it."

Robyn laughed, a soft tinkle that reminded him of wind chimes. "I'm definitely getting used to it."

He plugged into her gaze, and his heart knocked against his chest so hard he was sure she knew. "Looks like you'll need ice."

"The ice maker doesn't work." She glanced down at her ankle, swollen and bruised. "It really hurts, but I don't think it's broken. I've twisted it like this before."

"Can you take a pain reliever?"

"I don't think there's any here." She bit her lip, and her eyebrows drew tight. "I'll survive until I can make it to town."

He hesitated but forged ahead despite the quiet urge to stay silent. "Or maybe I can bring some back for you."

"No. You've done enough." Robyn shook her head before taking a long drink of soup, her face masked by the cup. No doubt on purpose. "I'll manage. I always do."

He took a sip, then set the mug aside. Somehow they had to come to a truce. "The hole over the porch is finished. Good enough to keep the rain off our new floorboards. Now they can be painted."

"Thanks." She stared into her cup, and her fingers anxiously toyed with the handle.

Silence settled between them, and he was unsure how to proceed now that he was out of pleasantries. While he wanted peace—craved it, even—Robyn was not in a place to accept him. He choked back a comment that would've sounded more like groveling. There was no reason he needed her approval or even her attention. He had enough to deal with, knowing that his job was on the line. Without the badge, he wasn't Caleb Sloane but someone else he wouldn't even recognize. Imagining life beyond the force kept him up most nights, and he didn't need thoughts of Robyn to complicate matters.

"Look, Caleb." Robyn spoke his name so softly that he had to lean closer. "I appreciate what you're trying to do." The wariness in her voice set him on edge.

"What, exactly, do you think that is?"

Robyn looked up and fixed her eyes on the ceiling the way one would in order not to cry. "Nothing. I don't know. Maybe you're just trying to be nice."

"You were lying on the ground." He tamped down the frustration starting to rear up. "Yes, I was trying to be nice. I've been trying all along."

"It's nothing personal."

How many times had he heard that? How long would one bad decision plague him? He stood. "Of course it is. What kind of man would I be if it wasn't personal?"

"This isn't a good idea." Robyn worried the cross on her necklace. "I really don't want to argue, but you've put me in the worst position. You have no idea."

He stalked to the door, then pivoted to face her. "*You're* in the worst position?"

Robyn's body went rigid, and anger hooded her eyes. "You have no idea what it'll be like for me to testify at the hearing. But let's not forget who you are and what you've done."

"Trust me—I never could."

"Then why did you come out here and pretend to be someone else? Why did you smooth talk me?" Robyn's voice warbled. "Why? So I wouldn't go to the review board?" Her eyes glistened. "It's almost unforgivable."

"Smooth talk you? I tried hard to keep to myself, until…" He shook his head, incredulous at her skewed ideas. After everything he'd done, she believed he only did it for self-serving purposes. Adrenaline iced his veins. "You're right. I have no business being here."

Robyn refused to meet his gaze. "Please, don't come back." Her words were only a breath.

There was nothing left to say. He stole a glance at Robyn before walking into the night. He'd shut the door, and now it was time to shut his heart.

Chapter Fourteen

Unshowered and sporting two days' beard growth, Caleb stormed into the café on a mission. After waiting for the gully to dry and getting a tow truck, he was itching to take care of business. The café buzzed with the morning rush, and the smell of cheap, greasy food wafted from the kitchen causing his stomach to growl.

He scanned the crowd until he found Phil, tucked away in a corner. Most patrons only gave a cursory glance as Caleb wove through the tables in the open-floored dining area, but the men at Dan's former table allowed their disapproving stares to linger. At this point, he didn't care.

"Thanks for returning my call." He didn't wait for an invitation to pull out a chair, flip it around and sit. At least Phil's secretary was amenable to giving out his whereabouts, which was the only thing that had gone right for Caleb all morning.

Phil issued a nervous chuckle. "Caleb, meet my client, Jarvis."

"Nice to meet you." He nodded at the town's well-known contractor. "This won't take long."

"I was just leaving." Jarvis tossed a ten-dollar bill on the table, said goodbye and found a livelier group to join.

"I'd ask what brings you by, but I have a feeling I don't want to know." Phil wiped his hands and placed his folded napkin over the remnants of a breakfast special.

Caleb rubbed his whiskers, an ever-present and rather itchy reminder that he hadn't been home in days. "It wasn't supposed to happen this way." His comment was a little too pointed. A little too loud.

"You've really let yourself go." Phil cast a furtive glance around the café and let loose with another stilted laugh. He leaned close. "You're causing a scene."

"Does it matter? Does any of it?" He motioned for the waitress to bring him coffee. After two nights of sleeping— if it could be called that—in his truck, he needed the caffeine. Once he'd left Robyn last night, he still hadn't been able to cross the gully, and it was too late to hike out and catch a ride at the main road.

"Of course it matters," Phil whispered tersely. "The chief is watching you from across the room." His eyes shifted toward the group near the kitchen.

Caleb schooled his face and posture. He had to at least appear stoic, even though fatigue was causing him to make irrational moves. It was like he was watching someone else's life unfold, and he was powerless to control it.

One moment had changed everything.

The rattle of the coffee cup as it settled on the table snapped him back to the present. He thanked the waitress and declined breakfast, even though the smell of sausage was overpowering. He only had a few dollars in his pocket, and he refused to bum cash off Phil.

"I've had back-to-back meetings. That's why I didn't call you yet." Phil reclined in his chair and crossed his legs. "You never said it was an emergency."

Caleb rubbed his eyes with the heels of his hands. He

drew a fortifying breath, wishing a hush hadn't fallen over the room just as he was about to speak. "I told her."

Phil whistled low. "I'm guessing she didn't take it well."

"That's the understatement of the century." He zeroed in on his friend. "You told me to just say it and that she'd be forgiving."

Phil held up his hands. "Wait a sec. I said she might. I made no promises."

The clang of dishes seemed to resume, and the chatter kicked up in volume. He rested his forehead in his hand, too exhausted and emotionally spent to even drink the coffee.

"Hey, this isn't like you." Phil gripped his shoulder. "You come in here like a wild man, mud on your shirt— this is more than things going badly at Lakeside."

"I was really falling for her." He nearly choked on the confession. It wasn't as though Phil hadn't known, but even Caleb was just now discovering the depth of his feelings, as though each layer was peeling away to reveal something new. "I guess I hoped maybe…"

"Maybe?"

Caleb looked up, his vision clouded with too little sleep. Too little hope. "I was thinking maybe she'd actually forgive me. That whatever was starting between us would continue." He shook his head. "I feel like a fool."

"Love does that."

Caleb snorted. "We never had a chance to get that far." A hard knot formed in his throat. "But I thought it could."

"She needs time. I'm sure it came as a shock." Phil drummed his fingers on the table. "Once she processes it, maybe she'll reconsider."

"No. She made it clear. I get where she's coming from." He couldn't figure out why or how she'd come to mean so much, so fast. "It doesn't matter, anyway. She's leaving once Lakeside sells." A slow ache spread through his gut. How would she ever finish getting the property ready? More important, how would he ever work out his promise if he wasn't allowed to help? And no matter how much he tried to convince himself it was all about the promise, now that he was banned from Lakeside he knew it was also about guilt. For all his talk about honoring Dan's memory, he almost had himself convinced that was the only reason. Robyn was right: he was deceitful. He'd even deceived himself. "You've got to find someone to help her finish restoring Lakeside. She at least deserves to walk away with something out of this ordeal."

Phil took a long, slow drink of juice. "No can do."

"There must be someone."

"I don't know anyone who'll do the work for free, and there's no money in the estate for it. I'm afraid she'll have to sell as is." Phil offered an indifferent shrug. "Of course, it'll be hard to find a bank that'll finance a property in that condition. Unless you've made a lot of progress."

Caleb attempted to mentally run through his bank account, which he'd steadily depleted throughout the renovation. What he had left he needed—if only for a small cushion. Of course, his figures could be off since he hadn't had a cogent thought in days.

He withdrew the crumpled dollar bills from his pocket and then rapped on the table. "If you think of something, let me know."

"Aren't you going to drink your coffee?"

Caleb stood. "Got things to do."

"I hope one of them is shower."

"You're a real pal." He stalked away and beelined for the chief's table, where he sat with a few of the officers. "Can we talk?"

Chief Warren's gray eyes shifted. "This isn't the place."

"You haven't returned my calls." Caleb hovered over him, arms folded, stance wide and firm.

The chief's hands fisted next to his plate, and his voice turned growly. "Make an appointment."

"Will do." Caleb nodded to his fellow cops before making a quick exit.

He hadn't done himself any favors by confronting his boss in public, but what else was he supposed to do? He'd been passive long enough by slinking off to Lakeside and hoping for the situation to work itself out while he ate guilt for breakfast, lunch and dinner. Meanwhile, he was about to lose the only thing in his life that mattered.

Caleb took a deep breath, filling himself with fresh mountain air and a new resolve.

If he was going down, he was going down with a fight.

"Stay off it as much as possible." Dr. Nelson gave Robyn a stern look—the same look he'd given her when she was ten and fell from a tree that she'd climbed too high.

"I will." She hobbled to the lobby, wishing the ankle tape was a bit looser.

Dr. Nelson followed her out. "So are you back for good?"

The question wound around her tighter than the tape. "I don't think so. The idea of staying was appealing, but it's not possible."

He leaned across the doorway, his eyebrows bunched. "You'll at least stay through the hearing, won't you?"

"Yes." A burning sensation shot through her at the thought of testifying against Caleb. When she'd promised Abby, she hadn't known. All she wanted was to do the right thing: to honor her dad. Why, then, did she feel like a traitor even though Caleb was the one who'd done wrong?

"I'll be there, too. I hear they're giving folks a chance

to have their say." He folded his arms. "You can bet I'll testify against that Sloane fella."

"Why?" she blurted before she could think better of it. A wrinkle formed between his eyes, and she quickly clarified. "Aaron Dirkson will be prosecuted, and I thought most people would think that was enough."

"Because we want to see justice done to everyone involved. Dirkson will get his due and so should the officer. Old Joe down at the hardware store told me a thing or two about his past and how Caleb used unnecessary force on Joe's son some years back. We don't need that kind of tough-cop business in Pine Hollow."

Robyn nodded, uncertainty flagging her conscience. She glanced at her foot. "Thanks for wrapping me up."

Dr. Nelson noticed Ginger across the lobby. "Ms. Hanson, it's been a while since you've been in. Isn't it about time for a tetanus shot?"

Ginger waved and disappeared behind her magazine until he left. "Honestly, the man still thinks I'm five. How'd it go?"

"I have to stay off it as much as possible." She tested each step as they left the office. Clouds obscured the sun, but the heat still blistered. "I don't know how I'm going to finish the repairs this way."

"Did you really think you could finish them without help, regardless?" Ginger's lips turned down, as though she were sorry to have to explain the obvious. "You're going to need a professional."

"I'll use whatever money was going to Caleb to pay the new guy." Ire rose inside her at the thought of Caleb profiting from the situation.

Ginger led her past the community theater toward the ice cream parlor. "I'm really sorry. I feel responsible."

"How is any of this your fault?"

"I should have known, but I've been out of town so much lately. When you told me there was someone working at Lakeside, I should've checked it out and made sure everything was on the up and up."

"I'm surprised you didn't recognize him." Because he was an unforgettable person. She shook off the thought and focused on how much he'd betrayed her.

"Pine Hollow isn't as small as it used to be. I know the people I grew up with, but the newcomers, not so much."

"Newcomer—meaning anyone here less than a decade?" She nudged her friend. "Don't be hard on yourself. You haven't done anything wrong. It's me. I was too trusting, and I let myself get carried away. How could I have ever thought he and I might have— Never mind. I can't even think about it."

"Why didn't he tell you sooner?"

"Wish I knew. He had no business being there in the first place. None of it matters now." She closed her eyes and basked in the sunshine, trying to soak in the moment for what it was. God had a reason for what she was going through. She had to believe it, or she'd fall to bits.

The ring of her cell phone shattered the quiet. Abby. They hadn't talked since she and Brad had left with the rest of the furniture.

She winced, then stepped away while Ginger window-shopped. "Hi, Abby. How are you?"

"Good. I wanted to get in touch with you before I come back to town. Brad and I have gone over the statements, and we wrote what we want you to say."

Robyn narrowed her eyes. Deciding to testify with them was one thing. Being told what to say was wrong in too many ways for her to get into over the phone. Make peace. "I'd love to get together to talk about it."

"I'm in Phoenix right now. I've been doing a lot of back and forth. This week the kids needed me here at home."

A dull ache formed in her heart. Would she ever know her nephews? At the funeral, she'd noticed the twin boys and realized how desperately she wanted to know them and to be known by them. But in her heart, she knew they were separated by more than distance. "I understand. Whenever you come back, I'll be here."

"For now, I'm going to email it to you." She sighed, long and slow. "How are things going at Lakeside?"

Abby was finally making something akin to conversation, and this was the one question Robyn couldn't really answer. "It's moving along. I took a little spill, so I have to stay off my feet for a while."

"Sorry to hear that." The line went quiet. "Maybe when this is all over, we can put the past behind us."

A jolt of happiness surged through her. "I'd like that. A lot."

Maybe her dreams for reuniting with her family weren't so far-fetched. If only she could get through the hearing. She closed her phone, then walked back to Ginger, thinking over the situation. Yes, the possibility to reunite with Abby existed, but to do so she'd have to testify against Caleb. And while she was angry with him, she couldn't deny the fact that her heart was ripping in half.

Chapter Fifteen

The chief was shorter than Caleb by a full head, but he carried himself like a bulldog—one who'd just had his bone stolen. When the chief closed the door to his office with a decisive thud, dread began to eat a hole in Caleb's confidence. "Thanks for seeing me, sir."

Chief Warren grunted in Caleb's general direction. He slung his leg over the corner of his desk and folded his arms. "I don't know why Sue rearranged my entire schedule for me to meet with you since there've been no new developments."

Caleb made a mental note to bring in a box of Mrs. Jones's donuts for the receptionist. "I want to know what to expect at the hearing." He remained standing, knowing the invitation to sit and make himself comfortable was not coming.

"Truth is, I don't know." The chief stared out the window and grumbled. "There's no precedent for this situation. We're working through it the best we can as we go along. Not that we're making you a guinea pig."

Caleb wasn't so sure. "Who's on the review board? At least let me know what I'm up against."

Chief Warren rested his gaze on the ceiling, as though

hoping for an extra shot of patience. "That's really not a good idea. This whole situation is already a PR disaster. We don't need you pestering the members of the board. That's against protocol."

His gut clenched. None of this sat right. There had to be more information available than what they were giving him. "Fine, I understand. What *can* you tell me?"

"It's a five-person panel, made up of civilians and members of the force. The mayor appointed the civilians, and I chose the officers. None of them work directly with you, so they can be objective." A placid look settled on the chief's face. "You might want to get a statement ready, because I think there'll be time for that. I heard they're planning to let members of the public speak, as well."

Caleb pulled in a breath that did little to calm him. He searched the chief's eyes, hoping to make a connection. "I care about his job. It's the only thing I ever wanted to do. I'm third generation."

"I've heard about your father. Sounds like he was a fine cop. What happened to him was tragic—caught in the middle of a Flagstaff bank robbery." The chief shook his head, uncrossed his arms. "Look, Caleb, you and I have had our differences over the years, but no one wants to see a fellow officer go down. The whole thing is convoluted, and I'm in a bad spot."

Not as bad as mine. Caleb remained quiet and hoped the chief would fill the silence. More than that, he hoped the review board wouldn't have access to the report that set his and the chief's relationship off to a bad start in the first place. He'd only been on the force a few months when he was accused of using excessive force. Thankfully the truth had come out, and the situation was chalked up to a rookie mistake. But it was a mistake that would shed a bad light on the current situation and call his judgment into question.

"You can't imagine the pressure on me to get this right. The politics involved…" Chief Warren rubbed his forehead. "Fine. I'll give you the names, but whatever you do, leave them alone. Am I making myself clear?"

"Yes, sir." Caleb nodded as he shot up a silent prayer of thanks. The chief rummaged through a short stack on his desk and came up with a printed copy of an email. Caleb scanned the names, and it didn't take but a split second for one to stand out. Joe Foster—Old Joe from the hardware store. The one man who'd been after him for years—the man whose son he'd been accused of using excessive force on during an arrest. An arrest that led to the first formal inquiry of his career. A flash of heat swept through his body, and he waited for it to pass before he offered the chief his hand. "Thank you, sir. If you think of anything else you can tell me, you have my number. I can see myself out."

He expected relief to filter through him when he closed the door, but instead his chest tightened. Too much anxiety. If this wasn't enough to get him back into church, nothing would be. He needed the prayer, the fellowship. The backup.

He stopped in front of Sue's desk and rubbed the fatigue from his eyes.

"Are you all right?" Sue peered over the rim of her glasses. "You don't look well."

"I'll survive." He pocketed the email and attempted to look confident and self-assured—anything but what he actually felt.

"We sure miss you around here." Her eyes filled with sympathy. "I'm looking forward to the day you get to come back."

Caleb scrounged up a smile. "I appreciate that, but it looks like I have more hurdles to jump before I get to wear my badge again."

"So I've heard." She leaned over her desk and whispered, "But there are more than a few of us keeping you in our prayers." Then she nodded, as though she had an inside track.

He thanked Sue and hurried out of the office, certain that God was trying to get his attention. It was time to set aside his issues. Time to hold his head up, and show the town he had nothing to hide. Regardless of the stares and murmurs, and whatever discomfort he'd have to endure, it was definitely time to get back to church.

Caleb took the next two days to convince himself to walk into the sanctuary. He came after the service started and slipped into the last row next to Phil. The moment the last amen was said, he stood and headed for the doors.

Phil caught him by the elbow. "Hold on. You can't just run out."

"Watch me."

"You said yourself that you need to get back into the swing of things, and this is part of it. At least say hi to Pastor Steve."

He hated when Phil was the voice of reason.

"Caleb." Pastor Steve lengthened his stride. "It's good to see you. It's been a while since you've been here."

"It's good to be back." He scanned the crowd, wary of the attention. A few offered smiles, but the men he knew to be Dan's friends shot cold, blank stares. So much for fellowship. He wiped his palms on his slacks.

"Sorry I wasn't able to be more help the other day with your truck."

"No sweat. The tow truck was able to get me out."

Pastor Steve leaned in close, his gaze reassuring. "I want you to know that I've had my ear to the ground about your hearing. We're praying for you, buddy."

"Caleb, it's good to see you here." Mrs. Jones tapped Pastor Steve on the shoulder. "Can I get a minute with you before you leave?"

"Sure, Ida."

Caleb shot another glance beyond Pastor Steve and Mrs. Jones to a woman desperately trying to wave the older woman away from the pastor. A woman who was doing her best to remain at least partially hidden behind a church bulletin.

Robyn.

How had he not thought ahead to the fact she might be at church?

For an instant, they locked eyes, and in her gaze, he saw a gamut of emotions that scratched the surface of his heart: anger, sadness, disappointment.

Caleb swallowed and looked away, his conscience not yet ready for another beating.

Fellowship was definitely overrated.

Robyn fanned herself with the bulletin, pretending to be indifferent, though she was anything but when Mrs. Jones invited her to church the day she stopped in at the Tasty Pastry. It never occurred to her that Caleb would come, too. Judging by the knowing glint in Mrs. Jones's eye, she wasn't the least bit surprised.

"I'll see you later, Pastor." Caleb's voice, low and mellow, caused her to glance up and notice things she didn't want to, like the breadth of his shoulders and his casual stride that hinted at confidence without arrogance. When he left, he didn't look back, and it bothered her that she cared.

"Sorry to have interrupted you, but Robyn wanted to talk to you before you left." Mrs. Jones ushered her forward.

Pastor Steve's smile widened under the fullness of his beard. His easygoing demeanor set her at ease. "It's nice to meet you. We had some great talks, your dad and I." Pastor Steve motioned toward the foyer. "Go grab some coffee, and I'll be out in a minute."

Mindful of her ankle, Robyn hobbled to the foyer, half hoping Caleb was gone and half hoping everything he'd said was a big misunderstanding. Near the coffee table, Phil had Caleb corralled between the wall and the coffee urn. The circles beneath his eyes certainly matched her own, and he appeared deflated compared to what he'd portrayed inside the sanctuary when he'd noticed her hiding behind the bulletin.

The urge to run away ballooned inside her, but she was determined to hold her peace. To be civil. And to douse the flame of attraction that had no right to burn. She edged closer to the table but couldn't reach the cups. From the corner of her eye, she saw Phil clap Caleb on the back and walk away, leaving them alone at the table.

Tingles danced up and down her spine as she searched for something to say. "I hope you understand why I can't have you at Lakeside." She uttered the words softly, so as not to attract attention.

"I do." He inched toward her. "Someday I hope you can hear me out."

She shook her head, then shot up a silent prayer. "Maybe. I don't know." Slowly, she turned to face him, afraid to look into his eyes and expose her feelings, ones even she didn't want to acknowledge. "Look, I don't think you're the awful person half the town is making you out to be, but that doesn't mean I can forget what happened."

"Understandable." He handed her a cup from the stack next to him. "Neither can I."

Tears pricked her eyes as he walked away, but she quickly composed herself.

"Sorry about that. A little church business." The pastor came up behind her. "I've been wanting to meet you. I was on a missions trip when your dad had his accident. It blew me away." Pastor Steve pressed the tab on the coffee vat to fill the cup and then handed the mug to her before starting on another one. "I would love to have done his service. I'm sorry I wasn't here." He shook his head, as though absorbing memories one at a time.

Robyn swirled a copious amount of cream into her drink, mostly to buy a few moments. She was still shaken by Caleb's presence, and she hesitated to discuss such private matters while people milled about the lobby. Seeming to sense this, Pastor Steve nodded his head toward the door. He led her outside, into the sunshine.

Wind moaned through the pine trees. She scanned the parking lot for Caleb's truck, but he'd already left—as well he should, all things considered.

"How are you doing?" The sincerity of the pastor's gaze added meaning and depth to his simple question. Though he was a stranger, she didn't feel wary talking to him, especially since he might be the only one with the answers she sought.

She fidgeted with her cup, directing her attention to the rising steam. "Not well. I mean, better in some ways than I thought I would be but worse in others. I've never lost someone close to me. Although, I suppose you know my dad and I weren't close."

"He mentioned that." Pastor Steve's words held no judgment. He nodded to a couple as they left the building and then rocked on his heels.

Emotion constricted her throat, though she couldn't name which one. Regret—or maybe it was relief. Right now, it was a fine line separating the two. At least her dad had talked about her, and that was a good thing. Unless the conversations were about how much she'd let him down.

She closed her eyes and allowed the sound of the cars on the road and the song of the birds to bring her back to the present. "I always believed I'd have time to make amends." She waited a beat to gauge Pastor Steve's reaction. "But that's the thing. We think our time is unlimited and that we'll have as long as we need to get it right." Tears brushed her eyes. "And it just doesn't work that way."

"It's a hard lesson." Pastor Steve pocketed his hand and sipped his coffee.

She drank the coffee that was too warm for a summer day but a comfort she needed nonetheless. "My biggest regret is that he died without knowing I still loved him. That I still wanted to be part of his life." She looked up at the pastor, desperate for words of absolution. "Do you think he knew?"

Pastor Steve's mouth tightened, and the grim lines around his eyes said he was trying not to hurt her feelings. Her stomach bottomed out like she'd fallen into a deep, dark pit. She pulled her gaze away and tried to hide her tears. This wasn't at all what she'd expected.

"It's hard to know what was in another man's mind." Pastor Steve guided her toward a bench that offered a bit more privacy. "Just like it's hard to know what was in his mind, I'm sure it was hard for him to know what was in yours."

Robyn nodded, doing her best to keep her composure.

"But what I do know is that he wanted to reconcile as much as you did." Pastor Steve lowered his voice as more people exited the church, chatting away like all was right in the world. Which, of course, she knew it wasn't. Pastor

Steve leaned forward, elbows on his knees. "He said he didn't know how to find you."

"That sounds about right." She cleared her throat, pretending to be more in control of her feelings than she really was. "My mom and I moved around a lot. We were never in one place longer than a year, until I was out on my own. I was surprised the lawyer was able to find me when Dad passed."

"He probably had more tools at his disposal than Dan did. He sure talked about you, though."

Good or bad? She was afraid to ask.

"It sounded like there were other complications that kept you two apart. Something about your mother, maybe? He never did specify."

"You don't know much more than I do." She tried to keep her tone light by forcing a smile.

"I know that Dan missed you. He always wondered what became of you." Pastor Steve appeared to be rummaging through his thoughts for more. "He wanted to know if you were happy. He said that after he became a Christian, he had an even greater desire to know you again, but I think his wife would've frowned on it."

Robyn sighed with relief. So he *had* become a believer. At least she had a future hope to cling to, though it did little to assuage her guilt in the present. She took another sip of coffee. "I wish I knew if he'd forgiven me. I was terrible to him the last time we were together."

Pastor Steve drained his cup. "We all do things we're sorry for, even if it takes years to realize that we've hurt someone. Or we might even realize right away. In the big scheme, what matters is what we do after the fact and how we treat one another going forward."

Fresh tears stung her eyes. "That's the problem. Even once I realized, I didn't act on it."

"It might be too late to get Dan's forgiveness—though it never sounded to me like he carried a grudge—but it's not too late for God's. He's the only one who can give you peace."

She nodded eagerly, the pastor's words a balm for her troubled soul.

Pastor Steve stood and walked toward a mud-caked truck parked next to the building and unlocked the door. "I have an appointment, but I'd like to talk again. Just remember this—we can't control whether or not an imperfect person will forgive us, but we can offer that gift to others." He climbed into the truck and rolled down the window. "I'll be praying for you."

In that moment, caught between memories of her father and anger toward Caleb, she could no longer ignore the relentless tug on her heart.

Chapter Sixteen

The circular saw was heavier than it appeared, at least after lugging it up two flights of stairs on a bum ankle. Robyn followed the signs until she came to a suite in the corner of the building with Phil's name outside the door. She shouldered her way into the office, where a receptionist greeted her with a puzzled expression.

"My name is Robyn. I have an appointment with Phil." She set the saw on the floor and waited until Phil opened the door and ushered her inside.

"What on earth did you bring me?" He adjusted his wire-rimmed glasses.

"It's not for you." She paused for a deep breath, vowing to ramp up her workout regimen. "It's for Caleb." Even saying his name churned up emotions.

"Aah." Phil flashed her a knowing look.

She shifted the saw from one hand to the other. "Where should I put this?" She glanced around the sparsely furnished room, which she surmised was left that way to accommodate the electronic golf game she spied against the wall.

"You can leave it by the door, for now." Phil moved behind his desk and motioned for her to have a seat. "What can I do for you today? I'm sure you didn't come all this way to show me Caleb's saw. I've already had the pleasure numerous times." He winked.

Robyn laughed, refreshed by Phil's lightheartedness. She settled into the chair and smoothed the hem of her sundress. "I have questions that only you can answer, though I've debated whether or not to even ask." The answer would be for her own peace of mind—nothing more, nothing less. "I need to know when my father updated his will."

Phil's eyebrow peaked. He turned to his computer and jiggled the mouse. "It's an old will, from before I was his lawyer."

That's what she was afraid of—her father had simply forgotten to change it. She forged ahead, determined not to come unglued.

"It's airtight, so no worries on that front. What else?"

"I'd like to know how much money is left for the renovations. I remember you said there wasn't any life insurance, but obviously there was some money for the property to start the renovations." She looked away, not wanting Phil to read her. "I need to know what I'm working with before I hire someone else."

"That one's easy—nothing."

"Nothing?"

"Nothing." Phil turned his palms up. "There never were any provisions. I'm sorry to say it, but the only money you'll get is from the sale of the property, assuming you get a good price."

"I should've known." No wonder Dad had left the place to her—he hadn't wanted to saddle Abby or Brad with the financial responsibility. She closed her eyes and massaged her temples. "In that case, how much do I owe Caleb?" The idea of forking over good money to him burned.

Phil pulled his hands away from the keyboard and swiveled to face her. "You don't owe Caleb a thing, except maybe a little understanding."

She allowed Phil's words to sink into the places of her heart she didn't want to examine. How many different directions could she be pulled and still remain in one piece? She sat taller, refusing to shrivel in front of Caleb's friend. "I think it'd be better to pay him."

"He never wanted money."

"What, then?" Her voice rose. "He was only fixing up Lakeside to make himself look good, wasn't he?"

"If you believe that, then you don't know Caleb." Phil's voice was as soft as hers was loud, and he spoke without judgment.

"I know enough." She stood and pivoted away from the lawyer's probing gaze. She had to get out of here and spend some time alone to process her conflicting thoughts. Naturally, Caleb's friend would back up his claims, so she simply couldn't trust him without further proof.

"Don't you realize? He was there for you."

Robyn stopped but refused to turn around. What did she believe? If she allowed herself to entertain the idea that Caleb was not as bad as he seemed, she could never go through with testifying at the hearing. And if she didn't do that, she had no chance at a relationship with her family. She'd waited too long, and this was her last shot. Sweat beaded her palms. "What do you mean?"

"Let me start from the beginning. Caleb made a promise to your dad." Phil's words hit their mark.

She turned to face him, working to keep a stoic expression. "He mentioned that, but he didn't give me details. Or maybe he did, and I wasn't ready to listen."

"That's understandable, and knowing Caleb, he didn't want to upset you any more than you already were." Phil leaned forward against his desk, balancing on his fingertips. Though his glasses sat too low on his nose and his tie was askew, sincerity shone in his face.

"I'm really not sure I want to hear this, even now."

"That's your decision. But rest assured, Caleb working at Lakeside had everything to do with following through on a promise to your father, because that's the kind of man he is. I had a hard time believing it at first, too, but one thing I know for sure is that Caleb Sloane is not a liar." Phil walked around the desk and sat on the edge.

"That's still no reason not to be honest with me from the start."

Phil tilted his head. "Do you remember the day Brad came to Lakeside and tried to intimidate you? Tried to ask you about some kind of files?"

She nodded, the memory assaulting her even now.

"Caleb knew you'd make him leave if he told you who he was, but he also felt like Brad was a threat to you. He thought you'd be safer with him around and that his promise to your dad would be better fulfilled."

The words rang true. The way he'd practically hovered over her whenever Brad was around and how she'd felt much safer with Caleb close.

"He's also the kind of man who'd never think to tell you he was not only working on the cabins for free but also footing the bill for the supplies. He knew you were on a limited budget, and there was no other way the repairs would happen because no one else would work for free. You'd never get the place in salable condition. Again, it all went back to his promise to do whatever he could for Dan." Phil's words wrapped around her conscience like a boa constrictor, tightening and leaving her without an inch to argue.

She licked her lips as she desperately searched for a comeback, a way to make Caleb the bad guy. But she couldn't. "If he's really the man you say he is, then he'll have no trouble with the review board."

"I never mentioned the review board." Phil folded his arms. "But since it's on your mind and you brought it up, I wish I were as confident as you. As much as Caleb has done for this town, people are not taking the situation lightly."

"Why should they?" She pointed to herself. "My father is gone because of him."

Phil held up a finger. "No. Because of Aaron Dirkson— a troubled teen who Caleb tried to help." He paused and began to pace as though they were in a courtroom and she was the lone juror. "When it came to light how rowdy the kids in town were getting, Caleb decided to do something about it. Did you know—" he stopped and faced her "—he somehow found the funding to start a youth center? Just to give the teens a safe place to hang out and keep them out of trouble."

"He told me about the youth center, and like I said, I'm sure Caleb will come out on top when it's time for the hearing." What she wasn't sure of was how she felt about it. No wonder Abby had said the process would be hard. Even harder for her, now that the cop wasn't a faceless person. "I can't see that he has anything to worry about," she said to convince herself as much as Phil.

"I'm sure you've already guessed your father was well liked. As much as it seems cut-and-dried to me, not everyone feels that way. The opinions seem to be equally divided."

"There has to be more to it."

"He's made his mistakes, and no doubt that will come into consideration." Phil nodded slowly, as if watching the scales of justice weigh out in his mind. "But since you're giving a statement against him, I suppose that suits you fine."

"How'd you know about my statement?" She eyed him, searching for a clue.

"I keep my ear to the ground." His gaze never wavered.

"I have to leave." She headed for the door as fast as her ankle would allow. Discussing Caleb only heightened her anxiety. "Can you please make sure he gets the saw?"

"No can do."

"Excuse me?"

"I won't be seeing Caleb for a while, and I don't want the saw in here. It's not professional. I'm busy for the next several days. There's a concert in the park coming up soon, and I'm the lead violin." Phil squared his shoulders. "Rehearsals and whatnot. So if you don't mind…" He waved at the tool.

Robyn wrinkled her nose. "Fine." She hefted the saw and reached for the door.

"He's usually home this time of day," Phil called after her. "He lives on Mountain Drive. You'll see his truck out front."

She quickened her pace to outrun Phil's voice. But what she couldn't outrun, no matter how hard she tried, was the ever-present thrum of her conscience.

Caleb's feet pounded a steady rhythm against the pavement. A long run was just what he needed to clear his head—or at least that's what he'd hoped. Instead he'd ended up at the church, pouring his guts out to Pastor Steve. But there was little Pastor Steve could offer other than an admonition for Caleb to "forgive himself"—a phrase he didn't want to hear for the rest of his life. Then he'd spent time at the youth center, but the whispers rumbling through town had finally reached there, too.

He rounded the corner and increased his speed. A grove of trees shaded the single-story home he'd purchased a year after he'd joined the force. Funny, he measured everything in his life in terms of when he'd become an officer. It was the only measure he knew, and now he was about to lose it. A heavy weight crushed him day and night—every time he even considered what life would be like without a badge. And now that he had nothing to do with his days, the hopelessness he was already feeling intensified.

Despair had settled in his bones the moment Robyn kicked him off the property, and only now was he realizing how much he depended on the restorative work at Lakeside to ease his mind. Without it, the wait for the hearing created a heaviness that sat like a cannonball on his chest.

The closer he got to his house, the faster he ran. His breaths came in sturdy puffs, and beads of sweat flew from his body. His sole focus was to finish strong. The moment he passed the mailbox, he slowed to a brisk walk.

A movement on the porch caught his eye. He stopped and wiped the sweat from his face. Surely he wasn't seeing right.

Robyn limped off the steps toward a red SUV. He stared at her, dumbfounded, as though seeing an adrenaline-induced hallucination. What would she be doing at his house? The incongruence of the situation left him off-kilter.

Uncertainty flickered across her face. She hovered by the driver's side of the SUV, her mouth moving as though she wanted to speak but couldn't figure out what to say. Kind of like him. A breeze lifted the hair from her cheeks—cheeks that reddened by the second.

He stepped forward, slowly, so as not to scare her off. "I didn't expect to see you here."

Robyn gripped the door handle. "I didn't expect to be here when you got home."

Then why was she? No way would he be blunt enough to ask, but her presence begged the question. A thousand thoughts looped through his head, but none of them made sense. Sweat continued to pour off him, and his heart rate increased to a higher speed than when he was running. Rather than stand on the curb dripping, he wiped his face with his T-shirt.

"I have to leave." Robyn opened the door.

"Wait." He scrambled for something to say. Anything to keep her close. "You didn't tell me why you came. I don't suppose you'd want to come inside and talk."

Robyn's forehead wrinkled. "No, I wouldn't."

He chided himself for the stupid question. "I don't mean to be rude, but why are you here?"

"You left your circular saw." Robyn pointed to the front door of his house. "Phil refused to bring it to you, so I dropped it off myself."

He fought off a sardonic laugh. Phil the Matchmaker. Only in this case Phil was one hundred percent wrong. Which part of Robyn-never-wants-to-see-me-again did his friend not understand? He worked to slow his breathing. "Sorry you had to come out of your way. I don't know what Phil was thinking."

"He said he had to practice for some concert because he's the lead violinist." Robyn rolled her eyes, her mouth tight.

"That sounds like him." He folded his arms, unsure how to respond. The awkwardness between them was foreign, and it burned him to think how close they'd grown before she knew the whole truth. In another time and place, they could have had something special, of that he was certain. "Thanks for bringing it by. I'm sure there are a hundred other things you'd rather be doing."

"No trouble." Robyn started to wave her hand, then

seemed to catch herself slipping into easy conversation. She dropped her hand to her side. "I'd better go."

"How're the renovations coming?" He hated the desperation that laced his tone, but more than that, he hated that he wanted her to stay. Though they were separated by the front end of the SUV and a slew of bad decisions, he was close enough to see her eyes sparkle. Close enough to see how unsure she was of her own feelings.

Robyn looked away. "Terrible—I mean, a lot more slowly." She shot a glance at her ankle.

"Are you supposed to stay off it for a while?"

"Yes, but you know how that goes."

He imagined she wasn't even close to following the doctor's orders, but it wasn't his place to say so. Never really had been. "I'm sure Phil can recommend someone to help you."

She shook her head, eyes closed. "I already tried asking."

"But…"

The depth of her sigh was surprising. Slowly, she trapped him with a remorseful gaze. "I had no idea you were working for free, and there's no money to hire someone else."

"Did you really think I'd take money?" He palmed his chest, glad she finally knew the truth. Not that it was likely to change things between them.

"I, well…I didn't know the whole situation from the start. Remember, you lied to me?" Robyn's blue eyes cut like ice.

"I never lied."

"You allowed me to make certain assumptions, and to me, it's the same thing."

"Truce." Caleb held up his hand, too fatigued to argue.

"I know some people who can do the work cheap. Let me at least help you find someone."

"Didn't you hear me? There's no money. None." Robyn's eyebrows drew tight. "I barely have enough to buy supplies if that."

"What do you plan to do?"

"Why do you care?" Her soft voice floated on the breeze.

"I always have." He closed his eyes against the memory of Dan's last words. *Help me.* After Caleb had promised to do everything in his power, he was obligated. Not anymore, according to both Phil and Pastor Steve, but the sentiment still hadn't reached his heart. As far as he was concerned, the promise now extended to Dan's daughter, a woman who'd quickly found her way into his heart.

"I'll manage." Her determined expression defied the quiver in her voice.

"I'm sure you will." He mustered what probably appeared to be a crooked smile at best. He cut across the grass toward his porch, then stopped and looked over his shoulder. "But if you want me to find someone, let me know. I'll do whatever I can for you."

Robyn's eyebrows pinched together. "I— Never mind."

"What?" He gentled his tone, hoping she'd speak. He ignored the rational part of himself that said to give up and to ignore the woman who wanted to see him hang.

"Nothing. It doesn't matter." She opened the car door.

Caleb walked back toward the curb and berated himself for what he was about to say. "Look, if you still need someone," he paused, desperately wishing for a heart made of steel, "I can do the work." He drew a deep breath to fortify his courage. What was the harm in being completely honest? At this point, he had nothing to lose—not his pride, not his dignity. Not even his heart, since it was already too late. "I know it's not ideal for me to be at Lakeside, but you would see I'm not the crazed cop you make me out to be."

Robyn cast her gaze to the pavement. "I told you at church that I don't agree with what everyone is saying."

"I'm sure you've wondered if they're right."

"Maybe. Does it matter?"

"Of course it does. You're wrong about me, and I'd like a chance to prove it. You'll see who I really am. Let me come back." He took a step forward.

Robyn tilted her head and studied him. "At this point, I'd love free help, but what do *you* get out of it? You know I'll still have to go to the review board."

"And you know I'll do my best to change your mind about who I am." The review board wasn't paramount in his mind at the moment, but her good opinion was. He took another step closer.

"Then when all is said and done you'll still get nothing."

"That's where you're wrong." Caleb swallowed, allowing a smidgen of hope to seep through. "I'll get the satisfaction of fulfilling my promise."

Chapter Seventeen

Caleb took a bite of his buttery croissant and scanned the newspaper. A few joggers took to the street outside The Tasty Pastry, dodging the occasional car, and a couple of stores turned their signs from Closed to Open. Pine Hollow was off to a yawning start.

"You're quiet. What gives?" Phil pulled up a chair.

"Exhausted." The past few days at Lakeside proved draining. Too much time expended on winning over Robyn. Not enough time spent in prayer.

The scent of bread wafted from the open door. "That's the official story. What's the real reason?"

Caleb gulped his coffee before remembering how hot it was. "It's hard to work with Robyn and have to hide how I feel."

"Why hide it? Everything's out in the open now. You might as well shoot straight and tell her. Have faith it'll turn out right."

"Faith," he muttered. Given the choice, he preferred logic to faith, but it didn't keep him from reaching out and believing the Lord had good things planned. Or at least it didn't used to. He polished off the last of his croissant. "I already know what she's going to say."

"What, you're a mind reader now?" Phil unfurled the napkin and draped it across his lap. "You should've seen the look on her face when she was talking about you."

His heart warmed at the thought, but only briefly. "That doesn't mean she'll forget who I am."

"Give her some credit. I'm not one to get mushy, but you need to give yourself some credit, too."

Maybe if his job wasn't in jeopardy he'd have more confidence all around. He glanced down a side road toward the station where his fellow officers were likely gearing up for their assignments. Like he should be. His stomach curled— a feeling that was getting all too familiar. "I don't know why I'm even thinking about it. She's about to leave town, and I'm about to lose my job. Guess it wasn't meant to be."

"At the very least, you still might be able to persuade Robyn to put in a good word for you. Her testimony would go a long way." Phil forked a bite of his bear claw.

"I can't do that. She'd think I was using her. I won't go there."

"Yeah, but I'm sure you can find a way to sway her opinion." Phil's tone lightened, and his mouth tilted with a sloppy grin. "If you put your mind to it, I know you can win her over."

"Don't you have a clarinet to tune or something?"

"It's a violin, and I'll have you know I'm first chair. I have a solo in the outdoor concert next week." Phil cocked his head and grinned. "Now, about your relationship—"

"There *is* no relationship." He folded the newspaper. "She's talking to me, but not like before."

"At some point, she's going to realize you two are perfect for each other. Then she'll stick up for you."

He leaned back in the chair and watched the sun peek through the clouds. "Forget it. I told you that I don't want to use her for the statement."

"There's no using involved. If she sees what a great guy you are *and* she knows how you feel…"

Caleb picked at the lid on his drink.

Phil dabbed his mouth. "You have to tell her how you feel before she's gone. You'll hate yourself later if you don't."

His friend's words synced perfectly with the burn in Caleb's chest every time he thought about letting Robyn leave Pine Hollow without admitting his feelings for her were still strong. She'd probably reject him flat out. Worse, it might make her even angrier.

Except that behavior didn't match the person he was getting to know. She was gentle and peaceable, wanting to see the best in others—if her actions toward her half siblings were any indication. But what if confessing his feelings opened her up to the possibilities? It was risky, but he couldn't live with himself if he didn't at least try.

And Robyn Warner was worth the risk.

He shot up a quick prayer with the promise of more to come, then stood and patted his pocket for his keys.

"Where are you going?"

"To take a shower. I have to get out to the lake."

"You're the only man I know who'd shower before going to work on a rooftop." A knowing smile spread across Phil's face. "Don't forget your hair gel."

For days, Robyn had watched Caleb work harder than anyone she'd ever seen, while she laid low and sought relief from her conflicting emotions. After a lot of prayer, she decided the least she could do was find a way to pay him, even if it meant doing so after she returned to California and a steady paycheck.

Decision made, she followed the pounding of the hammer and spotted Caleb on the roof. She wiped her palms on her shorts, then started up the rungs. Wind rushed up the side of the house, causing the ladder to sway. At the top, she rose to full height on shaky legs and treaded carefully across the shingles.

"Caleb." She spoke softly so as not to startle him. When he didn't answer, she repeated his name louder but was drowned out by the repeated bang of the hammer. She approached him, wondering how he could work so close to the edge without the same queasy feeling she had. When she reached the far side of the roof, she crouched low to secure her position. "Caleb." She tapped him on the shoulder.

He jerked backward and whipped around, grasping her. She clutched his arms and pulled him closer, away from the edge. His eyes widened, and he yanked the earbuds out of his ears. "You startled me."

She swallowed, simultaneously noting the friction in his voice and the cool scent of aftershave rolling off him in soft waves. Her pulse accelerated faster than her thoughts, and she grappled for an intelligent response. Talking shouldn't be so hard. She slid out of his grasp and looked at the clouds and the treetops—anything but his dark, riveting eyes. "I called your name several times."

Caleb turned off his music and situated himself so close she could feel the flex of his muscles as he wrapped the cord of the headphones around the player. "What are you doing up here? Your ankle's not going to get better with you climbing instead of resting."

"I can't rest with you working so hard. That's kind of what I wanted to talk to you about." There was so much more that she wanted to say, but she'd never risk exposing the feelings she tried so hard to smother. Her stomach dipped and rolled. The sooner she could get off the roof, the better.

"You noticed I was working hard?" He turned his face to her, his mouth firm against the smooth outline of his jaw.

She hugged her knees to her chest and twined her anxious fingers together. "I've been thinking…" She fumbled, uncertain whether the rush she felt at her neck was the wind or Caleb's breath. No, he wasn't that close. It was only her imagination running away in a moment of desperation.

"Thinking about what?" Caleb slung his elbow over one knee, seemingly more relaxed and casual than she could ever hope to be in his presence.

And yet—

Sitting next to him on the roof overlooking Lakeside seemed to be the most natural thing in the world, as though she belonged here. As though they both did. But the feeling was quickly drowned out by the rush of her heartbeat and the sense that she needed to square up with him before he swung the hammer one more time.

"We need to figure out another arrangement." She let her gaze fall on a fawn that munched on a tuft of grass in the clearing. Thunder rumbled a few miles in the distance, and the animal darted away.

"I thought we had it all worked out. You said I could stay." Urgency tinged Caleb's words.

"You can. That wasn't what I meant, I…" She dared to search Caleb's eyes. An undercurrent passed between them, and she sensed that somehow they were both bound to Lakeside—to each other. She prayed for clarity, because surely she misunderstood, and the feelings coursing through her were now one-sided. A sprinkle of rain dotted her face and brought her back to business. "Do you mind if we talk inside?"

"Scared of falling?"

"Something like that."

"Let me help you." Caleb reached for her hand and

tugged her gently toward the ladder. "I'll go down first and hold it steady for you. Don't move until I get to the bottom."

Her skin tingled from his touch. She sat back from the lip of the roof while Caleb descended and waited for his call. She rolled onto her stomach, hands gripping the shingles, and felt for the first rung with her toe.

"Easy now. One at a time. That's it." Caleb coaxed her so gently it unnerved her even more. She doubled her efforts to focus on the ladder, rather than look down or listen to Caleb.

She stepped off the last rung where Caleb's arms circled around her, gripping both sides of the ladder. His chest at her back, she had nowhere to go, but within a fraction of a second he moved away.

"I probably shouldn't have gone up. I'm sure you didn't need me interrupting."

Rain drizzled, landing in dewy drops on Caleb's gelled hair. "Looks like I'll need to cut the roof work short anyway." His eyes prodded her. "You wanted to talk?"

She motioned for him to follow her to the porch. "Great job on the roof. I know it's a big undertaking."

"Aah, small talk." His lips hinted at a smile.

"I've been using you," she blurted before she could stop herself.

Caleb's eyebrows arched, but he remained quiet. Only the patter of rain cushioned the silence.

She gathered her courage and continued. "There's no reason you should be out here working for free. I only let you back because I couldn't afford to hire someone, and now I realize how wrong that was."

"I offered. Besides—" he paused as the floorboard groaned with his movements "—you can't use someone when they know what you're doing."

"It's still wrong. I have to find a way to pay you—even if it's after I get back home." The last word nearly choked her. There was nothing about the apartment above the surf shop that felt like home. Not the same way she was starting to feel about Lakeside. "Things are tight right now, but I can't have you work for free."

He took another step closer, and he dipped his head to meet her gaze. "No. Not another word about it."

"But—"

Caleb poised his finger near her lips. "I don't want your money."

She brushed his hand away, resisting the temptation to cling to it. To cling to him. What was wrong with her? This wasn't at all what she'd pictured, yet it was so much more. She backed away and leaned over the railing to catch her breath. "I have to find some way to pay for your work. You can't possibly think I want to be indebted to you." She hoped her statement didn't come across as harsh as it sounded to her own ears.

"I hadn't thought of that."

His footsteps sounded behind her, and she could feel his nearness, though she didn't dare turn around. Heat flooded her cheeks. "See, you'd be doing me a favor." What was she saying? Was she so stricken by a handsome face that she'd lose all common sense and reason? This was the man she needed to make a statement against—a statement that pricked her conscience but was by all accounts her ticket into her family. She couldn't be on the same terms with Caleb that she once was and still make peace with Brad and Abby.

"A favor?" Caleb leaned against the railing, his arms thick and strong—a detail she kicked herself for noticing.

He had to know how his presence affected her, and he was using it to his full advantage. Perhaps she'd misunderstood, and the tug on her heart hadn't been from God but a result of this ridiculous attraction that continued to fester. Caleb was coming off as a nice guy, but he was only trying to convince her how innocent he was. And she was taking it all wrong and creating more problems. All she'd wanted to do was be fair to him, wasn't it?

"Look, forget I said anything." She trained her eyes on the flagstone walkway that ran parallel to the porch, hoping Caleb would move away—far enough he wouldn't see the red stain she knew was crawling up her neck.

"How about this?" He shifted, leaning his backside against the railing and folding his arms. He tried to catch her eye, but she pretended not to notice. "Instead of paying me, you can donate to the youth center—when you have the money. In fact, donating time would be more valuable than cash."

That was good to know, considering she had way more time than money.

"Whatever you would've paid me can go to them. I know they've got some ideas for their game room, and they always need extra supplies for the afterschool program." Caleb's voice radiated passion, and his eyes sparkled. "I can't think of a better way to work this out. What do you say? Is it a deal?"

She nodded, not daring to speak. Caleb really was all that Phil had purported and then some. Confusion wormed inside her, warring against what she sensed to be the truth. Because if she admitted the truth, she might as well give up on ever having a relationship with her siblings.

She was desperately afraid to trust herself. She was afraid to trust Caleb. But more than anything, she simply wanted to believe.

Caleb's heart lifted when Robyn agreed to donate to the youth center. Though he couldn't understand the sudden change in her attitude toward him, he decided to take it as an answered prayer, giving him confidence to reveal his feelings. Of course, it helped that she easily grew tongue-tied and that her cheeks flamed like the Arizona sunset at the briefest touch.

"Then it's all settled." Robyn turned and hurried toward the door.

"Wait." His plea stopped her, but she faced away, casting only a cursory glance over her shoulder. His palms grew moist, and his pulse kicked up a notch. Admitting his feelings shouldn't be this hard—especially when he was certain she already knew. They'd already as much as told one another how they felt before the truth got in the way. "I wanted to talk to you, too."

Robyn rubbed her arms, taut under the sleeves of her gauzy yellow shirt. "Sure."

"You're not going to make this easy." He huffed—not quite a laugh, not quite a sigh. He rooted himself in place, refusing to go after her and risk making her feel cornered. "Will you look at me?"

"I'm not sure where you're going with this." From the way she rubbed her arms more vigorously, she knew exactly where he was going with it.

"I've been hoping to talk to you, but I didn't want to jeopardize my being able to come here." He choked down the fear rising in his throat and shoved his hands into his pockets. He willed her to turn around.

"You sound…serious." Robyn looked at him with an expression that shifted between anxious and hopeful until the crease between her eyebrows smoothed out and her hands dropped to her sides.

He launched into his point before he lost his nerve. "I have to get everything out in the open. Working here and pretending that I don't have feelings for you seems—" he paused to search for the right word "—disingenuous."

Robyn's shoulders hitched as though she'd drawn a sharp breath. Rain pattered against the porch roof in time with the beat of his heart. He waited for a reaction, for an affirmation that he'd done the right thing by exposing his emotions, but the seconds ticked by without a word from Robyn.

"Please, say something." Caleb swiped the back of his neck, suddenly feeling foolish. Had he misgauged her attraction? He was no expert, but he'd been sure it wasn't a one-way street. Still, he hadn't expected her to run into his arms after all that had happened, though he'd secretly hoped. "I couldn't keep doing what I'm doing without letting you know where I stand. I don't expect you're happy about it, given the situation, but I thought you deserved to know."

"I don't know what to say." Robyn rolled the hem of her shirt between her fingers.

"I didn't mean to make things more awkward than they already are." He sent up a quick prayer that infused him with boldness. "But I believe you sense what's happening with us. You might even be fighting it because of the part I had in what happened to your dad."

Robyn nodded, her eyes wet; though no tears fell.

"Does that mean you still feel it, too?"

She covered her mouth and nodded again.

Caleb stood inches from her. "Robyn, if I could go back and undo that day, I would." His throat constricted, and he took a moment to breathe through it. "I hope someday you can forgive me." A lone tear slid down her cheek, and he reached out and brushed it away with his thumb. "If that day ever comes, just remember that my feelings were real.

This isn't about review boards or free labor or a hundred other things you might be thinking."

She gazed up at him, her stark blue eyes open and honest. "I want to believe you."

"Then do. Because this—" he motioned between them "—is about a man and a woman who, under other circumstances, might have had something special."

Robyn closed the remaining distance between them and laid her head on his chest. He embraced her and inhaled the scent of flowers and rain, a scent that he'd come to think of as uniquely hers. He closed his eyes and committed the feel of Robyn in his arms to memory. If nothing else, he had this, and he savored each moment breath by breath, because there was only one thing he could be certain about: he didn't know what tomorrow would bring.

Chapter Eighteen

Robyn arrived at the Hidden Hollow Inn, uncertain how to tell Brad and Abby she wasn't sure about testifying against Caleb, but when her brother launched into the meeting, she lost her nerve. He handed her the most recent copy of the scripted statement, detailing what they wanted her to say. They wanted her to demand Caleb's dismissal and disparage his character, and they were counting on her to pull everyone's heartstrings. After they'd surprisingly called her yesterday and were finally including her as a family member, she hesitated to say anything that would ruin their newfound relationship.

When they finished discussing the hearing, Brad closed his folder and pushed aside his empty soup bowl. "That about does it. One more week to go and we'll finally see this situation set right." His nostrils flared.

"It can never truly be right. I think we all know that." Abby's face darkened, and tears glittered in her eyes. She pulled a tissue from her purse and gazed out the picture window overlooking the town square. "I miss him more every day. Right now I wouldn't even mind him preaching at me. It used to annoy me, but I'd give anything to hear Dad again."

Robyn rubbed her temples to quiet an oncoming headache. Did she dare voice her opinion and risk offending her siblings? A gentle tug on her heart refused to let her leave without saying something, so she drew a deep breath and forged ahead. "I agree we should speak up for Dad, but have we considered the possibility he'd want us to forgive?"

Brad leaned forward, hands clasped on the mahogany table, a storm brewing in his eyes. "Who, Aaron or the officer?"

She swallowed. "Both."

"I haven't met this cop yet, but after I get my hands on him, he'll wish he made a different choice." Abby patted her arm. "Forgiveness is fine—noble, even—but we also want justice." The slight edge in her tone crowded out any chance for dissent.

"Dad would want us to band together and do the right thing." Brad's dark eyes locked onto her. "He might've had a religious thing going at the end, but he cared about this town. He cared about the people, and he wouldn't want anyone else put in danger. Has Old Joe ever told you his story?"

Abby shook her head, disgust rippling her features. "Apparently, Officer Sloane used excessive force on Joe's son during an arrest. From what I gather, the investigation into that was closed. But if you ask me, it's a pattern, and someone needs to put a stop to him."

"I think Dad would agree." Brad leaned close, his breath heavy with the smell of garlic and vengeance. "We will not let his death be in vain."

A ball of dread formed in her chest and smothered her rebuttal. Robyn took a moment to compose herself, not willing to compromise her tenuous relationship with Brad over ill-timed words. At least they didn't know about Caleb working at Lakeside or they'd still be directing their anger at her. "More than anything, I want to do right by Dad." Though what that meant, exactly, she hadn't yet defined.

"Then we're all agreed." Brad stood and gathered his things, Abby following his lead, as usual.

Robyn pushed back from the table. All things considered, she didn't know whether to hug, shake hands or simply wave goodbye. Thankfully she didn't have to wait long before Abby reached out for a genial embrace.

Abby smiled with the same lopsided grin that won everyone over when they were kids. "*I'm* glad we're finally back together." She darted a glance at Brad.

Robyn squeezed Abby's arm. "I am, too. I wish it hadn't taken a tragedy to bring us back in touch."

"It's our fault, too." Abby's eyes softened. "The important thing is that we're together now, and we all agree on what matters."

Brad snorted so quietly she wondered if she'd imagined it. Before she had a chance to further analyze, he reached out and gave her a side hug, scrubbing away the lingering doubts. He probably felt as awkward as she did and was simply making the same mental adjustments. At least he no longer seemed threatening—the way he had been at Lakeside. Perhaps Abby had reasoned with him.

Robyn left the inn with a renewed confidence in where she stood with her siblings, though she was still unsettled about the scripted statement since she was more certain than ever that she didn't want to testify against Caleb. But what *should* she say? She ambled along the sidewalk toward the hardware store where she was supposed to meet him, until she spotted Pastor Steve in front of the bakery.

"Look who's here, Franko." Pastor Steve's pug yipped in response. "How're things going out at the cabins?"

"The repairs are great, but…" She bit her lip, stopping

herself from saying more before she had a chance to pray. She inhaled the smell of fresh bread drifting outside every time the door to the bakery opened. Mrs. Jones waved from behind the counter.

"I'm guessing there's still a lot going on in here." He thumped his chest.

She nodded. "Between remembering Dad, the renovations and Caleb's hearing—it's a lot to digest."

"You care for Caleb?"

Robyn cast her glance to the sidewalk, noting the way her pulse ratcheted up at the mention of his name. Was it that obvious to everyone? "It's hard not to care about someone who's done so much for me."

Pastor Steve merely nodded, not appearing surprised in the least. "He's a good man. I've been worried about him. How's he holding up?"

"It's hard to say." Her voice thinned, and the familiar ache returned. She wanted to give in to the blossoming feelings, but at the same time she didn't want to be disloyal to her father's memory.

"That man is carrying one heavy load." The pastor pulled a doggie treat from his pocket and fed it to Franko. "Yep, one heavy load. I hope someday he can forgive himself and move on. It wasn't like he acted maliciously or did something he knew would hurt another person. I know it means a lot to him that you allowed him back at Lakeside. I get the impression this is a big part of his healing."

Tears clogged her throat. "I'm sure my dad would have liked that." If only she'd known him well enough to be certain. Then maybe she could openly admit how much she'd come to love Caleb.

The thought jolted her—love. Was that what she was feeling? She sent up a silent prayer for clarity. Surely it was too soon for love, but what else could have such a strong hold on her despite a situation that defied anything more than casual friendship?

"Your dad would've been the first one to slap him on the back and tell him to quit being so hard on himself."

She nodded, unable to speak past the swell of mixed emotions that urged her to fight for her dad's memory and also to make things right. Make things normal. Whatever happened from this point forward, she knew with unshakable certainty that her life would never be the same as it was during her easy free-floating days at the surf shop and the beach. Her father's death had awakened something inside her, a desire to reconnect and establish ties and to build bridges and make peace. Only she had no clue how, under the circumstances.

She turned to Pastor Steve. "I wish I could have known my dad at the end. It sounds like he was a wise man."

"With a great sense of humor. It's no wonder people miss him, and no wonder they're looking for someone to blame. Glad to see you haven't fallen for it." Pastor Steve palmed her shoulder before he tugged Franko's leash and strolled away.

Obviously, the pastor assigned better motives to her than what was really in her heart. Could he not see how conflicted she was? That her emotions were shredded? In that instant, she knew she wouldn't take sides against a man who hadn't purposely done harm. He was guilty of a bad decision, but that didn't make him a bad person. Or a bad cop.

It sickened her that she'd almost been coerced into testifying against Caleb. It sickened her that she was so drawn to a man she had such mixed feelings about. But most of all, it sickened her that she'd be forced to choose between her family and doing the right thing in regard to Caleb—the only person out of everyone involved who had any integrity at all.

With the roof finished, the new door framed and hung, window screens replaced and a few more plumbing issues addressed, it'd been a productive few days. The only big jobs that remained were painting the cabins inside and out and landscaping. Caleb lingered for a while, enjoying the way Robyn was finally opening up to him, until it was time to head back to town to meet Phil for a quick dinner.

When they finished eating, Caleb opened the café and was greeted with a rush of fresh air. "I've never felt this way with anyone. When I'm with her, it's like I'm doing what I'm supposed to be doing—and that's saying a lot." He'd been so involved in reminiscing about his time with Robyn that he'd been able to successfully endure the whispers and pointed glances from the tables around them. He popped a peppermint into his mouth and meandered down the sidewalk.

Evening settled over Pine Hollow like a cozy blanket with lampposts glowing and the usual stream of cars slowing to a trickle. Families clustered in front of the ice-cream shop, and owners walked their dogs around the town square.

Phil pushed up his glasses. "I'm glad you finally manned up and told her how you feel. The truth is a beautiful thing. Yes, sir, a beautiful thing."

"That's awfully poetic." He didn't even try to contain the sarcasm.

"Must be all the rehearsals. It's bringing out the romantic in me." A grin lit Phil's face. "Hey, I have an idea. Invite Robyn to the outdoor concert this weekend."

"I can't. That'd be like a date. I have to stay in neutral territory, like sweating my brains out at Lakeside."

"There's nothing attractive about that. She needs to see you accessorized with something besides a hammer." Phil shot him an elbow. "What have you got to lose? If you don't take a chance, she'll finish up at Lakeside and leave. You'll never see her again."

His stomach cramped. For the past few days, he hadn't been able to think past the upcoming hearing, but what Phil said was true, and there was nothing he could do to stop it. "Hanging out with her has been great, and I know she's not as closed off to me as she was, but the problem is that even if I tell her how much she means to me, she's still going to leave—and take my pride with her."

"What good is pride if you're having dinner with me for the rest of your life?"

"Touché." The thought of Robyn leaving Pine Hollow opened a big empty place inside him. He paused in front of the community theater. "But where does that leave you?" He teased Phil, thankful for his good-natured buddy.

"If you introduce me to Robyn's friend—you know, the one with the long black hair—I'll do just fine." Phil reached for the door handle. "Hang out a second while I grab my sheet music."

Caleb wandered to the edge of the building near the ice-cream parlor and sat on the bench to people watch and consider Phil's idea. He'd do it. Asking Robyn to a concert would be a great transition, and with the close moments they'd shared recently, he had a strong feeling she'd say yes. He'd bring it up tomorrow.

A couple came out of the parlor, the man speaking with a terse voice that drew a sharp contrast to the quiet murmurs of evening. They seemed oblivious to the stares they drew and the way everyone stopped talking to listen to them.

"There *is* no more doubt." The man waved a paper under the woman's nose, which she swatted away. "I had it verified."

Caleb sat taller, recognition dawning—Brad and Abby. They were so involved that they hadn't noticed him sitting less than a couple yards away. From the bit he saw, he couldn't imagine how Robyn was able to overlook their faults. She really was amazing, and that made her all the more attractive.

"She's on our side. Why not wait until after the hearing? This—" Abby grabbed the paper "—doesn't really matter. Not yet, anyway."

His heart hammered with every word, and his fists clenched. It was clear they were talking about Robyn, and it was equally clear by Brad's venomous tone that he didn't like her and didn't care what Abby thought.

"Why are you going soft now? You and I agreed that we'd take action once we knew for sure. Now there's no more doubt, and even she can't deny it." Brad pinched the bridge of his nose, his disgust unhidden.

"Because, she's not as bad as you've made her out to be. Plus, we need her for the hearing. I'm telling you it's not going to be as easy as everyone thinks," Abby argued passionately, disregarding the crowd spilling out the door of the ice-cream shop. "Whatever you want to do after it's all over is your own business. Look, take a day to think about it, and we'll talk when you come back from Phoenix."

Caleb's stomach tightened. They were using Robyn against him, yet Robyn trusted and thought the best of them. Adrenaline pounded through his veins, but he restrained himself rather than hauling off and teaching Brad a thing or two.

"Oh, we'll talk, all right. I could tell right away she's not committed. And if we don't do something fast, she'll get to keep the money from the sale of Lakeside. That was *our* home." Brad leaned into Abby's face and punctuated each word with spite. "It doesn't belong to her, and we have the birth certificate to prove it. The minute I pulled it out of that box, I knew it was our ticket to getting Lakeside back. Now that it's all verified, we don't need her." He snatched the paper back from his sister. "She wasn't even his biological daughter. Did she think she could fool us forever?"

The revelation hit Caleb like a sucker punch. They had a birth certificate? He had no doubt that Robyn was unaware, and the news would devastate her.

Abby folded her arms. "You're wrong. We do need her, at least until the hearing is over. After that, you can do whatever you want. Just leave me out of it."

"What I *want* is to get her out of the way. She doesn't belong in our home. She's nobody to us!"

In a flash, Caleb stood before Brad, fist cocked. "Watch how you talk about Robyn. I strongly advise you to keep your mouth shut."

Brad knocked his arm away. "Mind your own business."

Caleb shoved back. Indignation roared through him. "She *is* my business."

Darkness crawled over Brad's face, turning his grimace to a sneer. "It may have taken a while, but I know who you are. You're the cop."

"So what if I am?" He drew back, and his breath came in sharp huffs. He flinched when someone touched him from behind. He turned and met Phil's questioning look.

"Man, what on earth are you doing?" Phil shot a glance over at the crowd that stood riveted at the scene.

A crowd that included Chief Warren.

Chapter Nineteen

Anxiety steamrolled his confidence every time Caleb tried to decide the best way to break the news to Robyn. There was no good way to explain that the so-called brother she'd been trying to reconcile with was ready to blow her world apart and that everything she believed about her life was a big fat lie. It didn't help that she rode to town with him, the gentle ring of her laughter and the scent of her coconut hand lotion filling the cab of his truck. It made the situation worse, not only because he was distracted but he didn't want to ruin their precious time together.

When they emerged from the hardware store late in the afternoon, an idea struck him. "Would you mind if we stopped by the youth center? I haven't gone in a while, and I want to see how the game room looks. It's right there." He pointed to the stand-alone building across from the courthouse, already coming to life with kids just out from school. Visiting the center would both buy him a few minutes to gather his thoughts and help him forget about last night's incident in front of Chief Warren. He had to keep his mind off what happened with Brad or he'd go crazy.

"I'd love to see it." Robyn smiled with an expression that reminded him of hope and sunshine, roping his thoughts back to the present. She placed the bag she carried into his truck and closed the door.

"There's a concert tomorrow." His casual tone belied the fast clip of his pulse. "Would you like to go?"

"Sure. It'll be nice to do something besides paint. I can't believe how great the cabins are starting to look. I'm really hoping Ginger finds someone to buy the property who'll turn it back into a resort. She mentioned special advertising she can do once it's listed."

Caleb smiled. If Robyn's fast-talking was any indication, she was nervous, too.

"Do you help run the center in your spare time?" She looked up at him with wide eyes.

"Not lately." The confession saddened him. Since the accident, he'd been more concerned about his own welfare than the kids'. He promised himself he'd get his priorities right when the whole thing was over.

"Fixing Lakeside seems to keep you pretty busy, but we're almost done." Robyn fell into an easy stride next to him.

In a rush of confidence, he reached for her hand and squeezed. His heart warmed when she didn't pull away. "What will I do with all my free time?"

"If I had to guess, I'd say you'll be back to work soon." Her voice contained a quiet optimism that offered strength to his weary emotions. Was it possible she'd take up for him? No, she had already determined her position, and he didn't dare hope for more. He had to give her the freedom to follow her conscience without pressure from him.

He led her across the street and down the sidewalk, weaving between skateboarders who waved to him as they went by. "I wish I had your confidence. I've heard most people feel the same way you do." Not to mention he'd made a buffoon of himself when he'd challenged Brad. If that didn't seal his dismissal from the force, nothing else could. It was long past time to come up with a plan B, but doing so was akin to giving up entirely, and he just didn't have it in him.

Robyn stopped. She seared him with a gaze that held feelings they had yet to fully express. "Did."

"Did?" He swallowed, hard. "Does that mean—" he paused to give the words a chance to work their way around the lump in his throat "—that you've forgiven me?"

Robyn glanced around and smiled at the teens teasing one another on their way into the youth center. She tugged his elbow until he followed her under the eaves. "This isn't easy to say. In fact, I'm not sure I should." Several moments passed before she continued. "I'm ashamed to admit it, but in a strange way I almost wanted to hold a grudge against you. It felt like forgiving you meant betraying my dad. You probably think I'm ridiculous."

Caleb ran his hand over the back of his neck, conscious of the kids coming and going. "I could never think that. You're trying to make the best decisions you can, and it's hard to know what to feel. Can I ask what changed your mind?"

Redness climbed into her sun-bronzed cheeks, and she cast her glance to the ground. "It didn't happen all at once. After a few conversations with Pastor Steve and a lot of prayer, I realized I was blaming the wrong person, and that forgiveness is the only way I can have peace. I'm really sorry."

Relief flooded him, and he savored her mercy. For a moment, the world seemed new and brighter, more full of hope. The forgiveness he craved was finally happening, but there was one thought he couldn't dismiss, a voice that had nagged him since the accident. "Do you think you can forgive Aaron?"

She stared into the distance, her features hardening for an instant. "It's a process. But I'd like to get there. Holding a grudge is hard work and only hurts in the end." She turned her probing gaze to him. "Have you?"

Her question pierced the tender place in his heart he tried to hide. How many times had he laid awake at night, mentally forcing all the blame that had been cast on him onto Aaron? He knew many people were logical about the cause of the accident, but there were many more for whom Aaron's arrest wasn't enough to satisfy their thirst for justice. Some days he hated Aaron. Then he hated himself for feeling that way.

"You don't have to answer. It's just something to pray about, and hopefully, one day we'll both get there." She caressed his arm, and pointed him toward the youth center.

Caleb opened the door for Robyn, grateful how much they'd come through—together. It endeared her to him even more. Despite the unfinished business he knew he had in regards to Aaron, he felt freer than he had in weeks. He took Robyn through the lobby and introduced her to the volunteers that ran the front desk and the director.

"Fancy seeing you here." Phil strolled out from the game room wearing a serious expression. "Good to have you back."

"We're just visiting. I wanted to show Robyn around."

"I need to borrow Caleb for a minute." Phil gestured to the beanbags on the floor. "Make yourself at home."

Images of last night bombarded him. The shocked look on Brad's face. Phil's gentle reprimand. Chief Warren shaking his head and walking away. That was almost worse than getting chewed out because then at least he'd know where he stood. At this point, he was left guessing, and his guesses always veered into worst-case-scenario territory.

Caleb strode behind the desk, determined to get the

conversation over with. The last thing he needed was a reminder from Phil how out of line his actions had been. The office door closed with a dull thud. "I don't want to hear it."

Phil slung his leg over the stool in the corner. "Better coming from me than getting blindsided."

He folded his arms and remained silent.

"Talk around town is that the committee has already made an unofficial decision on their recommendation. I don't need to tell you last night's performance didn't help."

"I always appreciate when you brighten my day." His jaw tightened, and he broke out in a cold sweat.

"I wanted to give you a heads-up, but I also wanted to make sure you're doing okay." Phil slid off the stool and made his way toward Caleb. "How'd Robyn take the news? She looks good for a woman whose world was upended."

"That's because I haven't told her about the birth certificate."

Phil groaned. "You said you were going to talk to her first thing."

"It didn't come up."

"Do I need to pin a note to your shirt? C'mon, man, you don't expect me to believe you forgot. Listen, she's bound to hear the truth sooner or later, and it'd be better coming from you. Didn't you learn anything about keeping secrets? Don't make the same mistake."

"Maybe it's none of my business."

"You don't really believe that."

Unfortunately, Phil was right. As much as he wanted to talk himself out of it, he knew Robyn deserved to hear the news from someone who cared about her—not from Brad. He uncrossed his arms. "What if Brad's wrong—or worse, lying? I don't want to say something to Robyn then find out we're wrong. Do you believe what Brad said is true?"

Phil's face blanched.

"No, man. You knew the whole time…"

"Not the whole time. But as the one handling Dan's estate, they came to me a few days ago with a birth certificate."

"Why didn't you tell me?" Caleb raked his fingers through his hair.

"Attorney-client privilege."

"I don't know why I expected you to help. Looks like I'm on my own." He stormed out of the back room, then did his best to paste on a placid expression. He grabbed Robyn's hand and pulled her out the front door, amid a chorus of goodbyes.

"Wait, I didn't get to check out the game room. Why are we leaving so soon?"

He pulled her around the side of the building where Rocky Lopez and his friends practiced tricks with little attention to anything but their boards. He drew a sturdy breath and tempered his tone. "I have something to tell you."

Robyn's eyes brightened with excitement. "I have something to tell you, too, and I have to do it now or I'll never say it." A smile illuminated her face, and she took a step closer, a mere breath away. "I feel the same way."

"About…"

"You—about what you said." She bit her lip and engaged his eyes. "As much as I tried to tell myself otherwise, I think you and I have something special between us. I know the timing is awful, especially since I don't have plans to stay in town. But you deserve the truth."

His heart blew up in his chest, leaving him exhilarated, slightly exhausted and utterly speechless. Robyn's confession made his news that much harder to deliver. He dreaded being the one to wreak havoc on her world—again.

She smiled up at him. "Now, what were you going to tell me?"

* * *

She'd done it—completely exposed her heart—and now she couldn't take it back. Not that she wanted to, but it was simply ridiculous to share her feelings when she knew there was no way they could pursue a relationship. And it didn't help that Caleb refused to respond.

She nudged his arm. "You said you had something you wanted to talk about." She prayed she hadn't ruined the moment. What was she thinking? She'd been so caught up in spending time with Caleb that she'd lost her common sense.

His neck bobbed. Slowly the shock left his face, and the corners of his mouth tipped up. "You caught me off guard—in a good way."

She clutched her chest. "You had me worried there for a second."

"My feelings haven't changed. Trust me."

That was the thing—she actually had come to trust him, which filled her with a deep peace. A sense of well-being that she had finally met a man she could rely on, who wasn't afraid of doing the right thing, whatever the consequences.

"Let's walk." He circled his arm around her shoulder and guided her to the rear of the building. The breeze picked up the scent of his spicy cologne, or perhaps it was hair gel or aftershave—she couldn't really be sure. The only men she knew smelled like sunscreen and surf. It was as though every experience with Caleb was brand-new.

Flowers hedged a small lawn behind the youth center, and a bench lined the wall in the shade. They sat quietly for a moment, and though they'd worked together with privacy for weeks, this was different. Everything was different.

"I probably shouldn't have said anything." She pressed her palms together between her knees.

Caleb fingered a stray strand of her hair before tucking it behind her ear. "Why would you say that? You can't imagine how much I've wanted to hear those words. To know that the attraction isn't one-sided."

"It's a relief to get it in the open." Her ear tingled where he'd grazed it. "It's just that…it can't go anywhere. I know that, but it's really hard to accept." She risked peering into his eyes and was met with genuine warmth.

"Now don't go breaking up a beautiful thing before it has a chance to get started." He slid his hand down her arm and twined their fingers together. How long had it been since someone held her hand? A simple gesture that thrilled her in a completely foreign and invigorating way.

"I think we both know why." She drew her gaze away.

"Because you're Dan's daughter?"

She whipped around. "No—not at all."

A trench formed between his eyebrows, and he shifted on the bench. "What, then? I can't think of a bigger obstacle. Are you concerned about what Brad and Abby will think?"

More than he could possibly know. She was desperate to rejoin the family, and the closer she was to Caleb, the less likely that would be. Especially if their relationship— if that's what they actually had now—came to light before the hearing.

She squeezed his hand. "Have you forgotten that I'm leaving as soon as Lakeside sells?"

"In that case, we'll have to make sure Ginger forgets to list the property." He emitted a tight laugh. While he was responding in all the right ways, the bounce of his knee and the slight tic in his jaw showed he wasn't feeling as smooth as he appeared on the surface.

She chided herself for reading too deeply. "When I first got to Pine Hollow and my brother and sister weren't receptive, I was ready to get the property sold and get out of here. But now…"

"Now?" He prompted her with a glint in his eye.

"Since today is full of true confessions, I'll admit that I'd love to stay. The place has grown on me—not just Lakeside, but the whole town." She gestured to the side of the building toward the sound of skateboard wheels rolling across the pavement. "This is a great place to settle down and raise a family." Her breath hitched. Hopefully the mention of family wasn't too forward, as though she were making premature suggestions.

"Pine Hollow has had its share of troubles, but you're right. This is the place to get married and raise kids." He ran his fingers down her back, sending shivers all the way to her toes.

"The troubles here are nothing compared to what we have where I'm from." She gazed up at him. "I can really appreciate that you're trying to keep Pine Hollow a great place. Look what you've done here. The youth center is amazing—what little I got to see." She leaned against him and stayed.

"The center is important to me in ways I can't fully explain. Even though the town is relatively peaceful, there's still more that can be done. More kids to help."

"Like Aaron?"

Caleb nodded, slowly. "Just like Aaron. I hate to say it, but that could've been me."

"I really admire what you're doing here." She resisted the urge to nestle closer, even though having his arm around her seemed so right and natural.

"Then stay. Help me. You can be part of the work."

Hope lit in her heart before reality snuffed out the glow. She pulled away. "Like I said, I'd love to stay, but I can't. There's no way I can afford to keep Lakeside."

"You don't have to live there. Find a place here in town. Get a part-time job somewhere."

"Part-time?"

"Sure, that way you could spend time here at the center with me." His grin dissolved her doubts, and for an instant, the idea of staying in Pine Hollow seemed plausible. Caleb leaned closer. "We can figure it out."

"We? I like the sound of it." What if it was possible? She didn't have to keep Lakeside to live in Pine Hollow. All she needed was a job and a cheap place to live. It really wasn't as complicated as it first sounded. For once, she wasn't afraid to hope.

Caleb's lips brushed her cheek. "Get used to it."

She smiled, enjoying the feel of his skin against her face. She could definitely get used to it, and she didn't know whether to be excited or terrified.

Chapter Twenty

"I'm going to do it. I'm staying in Pine Hollow." A thrill ran through Robyn at her announcement.

Ginger shrieked and reached out for a bear hug, nearly pulling them both off the dock into the lake. "That's a huge answer to prayer. Now you can take your time finishing the renovations since I won't be listing the property."

"Hold on. I still have to move out of Lakeside, but I think I can make a go of it in town, as long as I can find a decent job."

"What changed your mind? Wait, don't tell me— Caleb?" Ginger nudged her.

Robyn couldn't stop the grin from spreading. She swished her feet in the water in an effort to appear calm. "I'd be lying if I didn't admit he's a big part, but there's more to it. Pine Hollow is starting to feel comfortable. Don't get me wrong—I love the beach, too, but this is different. Somehow I feel like God's finally led me to the right place." She thanked God for the peace that rained down on her since she'd made her decision. He was her father, guiding her to where she was supposed to be.

"In that case, we still have some work to do."

"Yes, like cleaning out the boathouse. Check it out." She

stood and helped Ginger to her feet. She cut a path to the shack and pushed open the creaky door. "Does this bring back memories or what?"

A smile brightened Ginger's face. "Remember that day we went on the lake with those two guys, and we accidentally tipped the canoe?"

"I don't think we ever saw them again." She laughed as she crouched to finger the bottom of the small boat in hopes of finding the source of the leak. "All this stuff will have to go. No matter where I move, I won't be able to store it. Anyway, come help me get ready for tonight." She rose, a surge of excitement bubbling in her chest at the thought of her date with Caleb.

"I can't believe you're going to the concert together. What happens if your brother sees you?"

Dread swirled in her stomach, but she refused to give in to fear. "That won't happen. He and Abby are both in Phoenix until the hearing, and I'm not going to worry about it until then." She had two days to figure out how to tell them she was asking the panel to consider the good of the town instead of demanding Caleb's dismissal.

"Sorry, but they don't strike me as the understanding type." Ginger wrinkled her nose. "You shouldn't let them off so easy. If it were me, I wouldn't trust them for a minute."

"Abby has softened up. Maybe she can talk to Brad." She rubbed her temple against the throb that appeared every time she thought about the situation. "I don't want to lose my chance with them and the possibility of getting to know my nephews, but I can't walk away from Caleb. Not now." She dusted her hands and stood.

"What's this?" Ginger held up a book, a puzzled expression flickering on her face.

"I'm not sure. Where did you find it?" She took a faded leather Bible from Ginger and examined the cover.

"It was next to the vests." Ginger pointed to a shadowy nook next to the door.

Hidden in plain sight.

Robyn leafed through the pages with verses highlighted in many colors and bookmarks placed in multiple spots. At the end were notes…and pictures.

Pictures of Robyn as a baby, child and teen with captions and comments. The last few pages appeared to be journal-type entries, the most recent ones dated mere days before her father died. She saw only one word before tears blurred her eyes—*forgiveness.*

Her fingers trembled as she closed the Bible, too stunned to speak. Though she cherished Ginger's friendship, she wanted to savor each moment, each page alone. *Thank You, Father. You knew what I needed. You've always known what I need.*

"This is what you were searching for." Ginger offered a gentle hug before guiding her into the sunshine.

"How could I have missed this?" She swiped the moisture from her face, then clutched the book to her heart. Finally, the evidence she needed to put her mind at rest. "Why do you think it was out here?"

"Could be anything. Maybe he wrote in it early in the morning when he came down to the lake." Ginger flashed a hopeful gaze. "Or maybe he didn't want anyone else to find it."

She started up the path toward the house. "Do you see what this means? His leaving Lakeside to me wasn't a fluke or an oversight. He wanted me to have something. He wanted me to remember him." The sense of obligation that had hung over her since arriving was replaced with gratitude. Confusion with peace. "I wish there was a way for me to keep Lakeside, maybe even open it for business again—like it was when I was a kid. It's just not possible for me to handle a mortgage right now."

"I'm sure he was planning on having it all paid off before it ever went to you. It's a shame we can't think of a plan." Ginger tottered up the trail, flicking away the foliage that brushed her pantsuit.

"Maybe, depending on what kind of job I can find, and how soon…" Robyn cut herself off, afraid to get too excited. Still, she couldn't shake the notion she'd finally found her place in the world, a place to be herself and settle down. A place to call home.

"I'll start putting my feelers out. Maybe you could even get the loan restructured so you can handle it."

It wasn't likely, but she refused to let her doubts ruin the moment. This was what she'd been praying for, and now she had her answer. "You can't imagine how amazing I feel right now. It's like I'm starting a brand-new life."

"That's because you are. This is going to be great, but first—" Ginger caught her by the shoulder "—we have to get you ready for tonight. You don't want to keep Caleb waiting, even though it doesn't seem like a real date if I'm dropping you off."

"There's no reason for him to come all the way out to Lakeside when you're already here. Are you sure you don't want to come along? Afterward, the four of us could grab a bite to eat."

"Four?" Ginger's eyebrow peaked.

"Yeah. You, me, Caleb and Phil—he's first chair in the orchestra." She shot a playful elbow.

"Even if I didn't have a late appointment, I'm not interested in being set up." Ginger continued up the hill, casting a quick glance over her shoulder. "Besides, he's not my type."

Even without Ginger along, Robyn knew it was going to be a night she'd remember forever—not only because of Caleb and the direction she strongly sensed they were going but because for the first time in over a decade she felt her father's love.

Caleb broke out in a sweat. He shoved his hands into his pockets and tried to appear casual in case Robyn was already among the crowd gathering at the town square. Phil stepped off the platform and headed toward him.

He released a nervous chuckle. "Shouldn't you be making sure the orchestra is in tune?"

"Not when my best friend is down here looking absolutely panic-stricken." Phil plucked a string on his violin.

"You would be, too, if you had to tell someone they've been lied to their whole life. You were right. I have to do it right away, or she'll never trust me again." He scanned the crowd for the familiar sun-bleached hair and bright eyes. He also searched for the chief, Old Joe and anyone else he needed to avoid. "All I really want is to tell her how much she means to me and that I can see us spending the rest of our lives together."

"Slow down, bud. You can't go that fast. You'll scare her away."

"Good point." But that still didn't change his feelings, and it didn't change the fact he was holding a secret that he needed to get out before she heard it elsewhere. He folded his arms and widened his stance. "There's too much to deal with right now, anyway, starting with the news. According to her, Brad and Abby will be back tomorrow or the day after. I don't want her to hear it from them."

"At least wait until after the concert. You don't want to miss my solo." Phil returned the conductor's wave. "Looks like we're almost ready to start." He made his way through the crowd and up to the stage and then proceeded to tune the orchestra.

"There you are. I've been looking everywhere for you." Robyn brushed against his arm, sending a shock wave of adrenaline all the way through him.

"I've been right here the whole time." He drew her into a tight hug and savored the soft scent of coconut lotion that wafted off her before he remembered tonight's mission. It felt like hornets swarmed his gut. There wasn't enough time to talk before the concert started, but there was no way he could sit on a park bench right next to Robyn for the next hour and say nothing. He sucked in a tight breath to fortify his courage.

"Oh, good, I made it in time." Ginger waved as she strode toward them.

He swallowed a groan. How could he discuss a private matter with *her* around? Not that talking under the din of the milling crowd and the tuning orchestra was such a hot idea. What was wrong with him? He should've planned to meet earlier, despite Robyn's protests that she had to see Ginger at Lakeside.

"I'm glad you came." Robyn reached out to her friend.

"My client bailed on me, so I decided coming to the concert sounded a lot better than eating dinner by myself." Ginger motioned to the park bench. "Let's grab a seat before they're all taken."

Caleb rubbed the crimp in his neck. He sat next to Robyn and casually wrapped his arm around her. Then he proceeded to steal a kiss on her cheek.

A blush tinged her features, highlighting her natural beauty. She cleared her throat and faced Ginger. "Maybe we can all do something afterward."

A ripple of applause rolled through the crowd when the conductor grabbed the microphone. He took a quick bow, welcomed the audience and thanked them for coming out. When he introduced the first piece with Phil as the solo-ist, Caleb dismissed the nagging anxiety. There would be plenty of time after the concert to pull Robyn aside. He'd make sure of it. Plus it gave him more time to pray.

The crowd stilled. Members of the small orchestra took up their instruments, and soft music floated on the breeze. Robyn drew closer, the slight rise of her shoulders pressing against him with each breath. He reached across his lap and grabbed her hand, rubbing her fingers in time to the song.

A short break in the melody signaled the start of Phil's solo. The mournful trill of his violin mesmerized the audi-ence, and even Caleb refused to breathe while Phil's bow skipped across the strings. He played with intensity and emotion that shook Caleb to the core.

Robyn moved, catching his attention. He looked down at her, and their gazes fused in silent understanding, as though everything they'd gone through together had led to this one, beautiful moment. Her sweet breath swept over his face. His lips found hers, ready to explore and savor—

"Well, look what we have here."

Caleb jerked back, dumbfounded by the harsh voice cutting through the music.

Brad towered over them, meaty hands fisted on his waist. Abby stood next to him with her eyebrows drawn tight. She shook her head. "Robyn, what are you doing?" Her shrill tone drew stares.

Robyn closed her eyes. "Can we talk about this later?"

Blood hammered through his veins. What had he been thinking? He never should've come out in public with Robyn until he'd delivered the terrible news. "Robyn, there's something you need to know." He tried to keep his voice quiet, controlled.

She pulled back, eyes wide and trusting, then she flicked a glance at Brad.

"I told you she wasn't on our side." Brad's face purpled as he zeroed in on Caleb. "No wonder you picked a fight with me the other night."

"Fight?" Robyn sat up, alarm covering her features. "Caleb, what's he talking about?"

"Can this wait? Or can you go someplace else?" Ginger's hoarse whisper seemed to draw equal attention.

"She *was* on our side. This must've been part of his brilliant plan to get to her before the hearing." Abby shot a vengeful look, which softened only a little before landing on Robyn. "Don't tell me you fell for it."

"You're both out of line." Caleb rocketed off the bench, ready to remind Brad exactly how badly he'd been outmatched the other night.

A smug expression settled on Brad's face. "*We're* out of line? You're the one who duped my so-called sister."

Robyn rose, her eyes wide and vulnerable. "Brad, what are you talking about? I thought you were finally accepting me." She clutched her chest with a hopeful expression that ripped Caleb's heart.

"Get real." Brad's forehead crimped. "You're no more our sister than her." He motioned to Ginger. "Or didn't Prince Charming tell you? Go ahead and ask him."

The music stopped.

A polite, disrupted applause trickled through the crowd. Heads turned, and then the whispering started. Ginger groaned and shielded her face.

"I don't understand." Robyn's gaze volleyed between him and Brad. "Someone better explain right now. What do you mean I'm not your sister?"

"We found your original birth certificate in those boxes we picked up." Abby's shoulders slumped as she fidgeted with her purse strap. "There's someone besides our dad listed as your father. I'd heard my mom mention it years ago, but I didn't think it was true. Brad thought you knew and were trying to take advantage of us, but I told him there was no way."

Tears trailed down Robyn's cheeks as she turned her attention to him. "And you knew about this?"

His heart dissolved when he reached for Robyn, and she shook him off. He shoved his hand inside his pocket, dejected. "I just found out. That's what we argued about."

"Why didn't you say something?" Her voice quivered. "Why?"

The question ricocheted in his head. There wasn't a good answer, only excuses. He strained for a reason that would ease her disappointment and pain, but all he was left with was the feeble truth. He lowered his eyes. "I was planning to tell you tonight."

She pointed at him. "That's not good enough. And you know what? I don't even want an explanation." She started to walk away and then stopped to throw one last glance over her shoulder. "Please don't come around again. I'm done."

Hope shriveled inside his chest as he watched her walk away. The music resumed, and Brad, Abby and Ginger were gone.

For more than a month, he'd been waiting for the final blow, the one that would knock the life out of him and call him to account. The town of Pine Hollow wanted justice, and this was the turn of events that doled it out.

Because right now, even without the hearing and the rendering of a formal verdict, he was getting exactly what he deserved.

Chapter Twenty-One

Even after a night of tears, prayer and heartache, Robyn hardly knew whether to feel worse about losing the man she was falling in love with or losing her identity. To be robbed of both in one shot gutted her already wounded spirit.

She dragged the rented paint sprayer out of Ginger's SUV and headed inside Joe's Home and Hardware. Forget painting the cabins. What was the use? She refused to put any more effort into the property, because pouring out her soul hadn't been enough. Somehow Ginger would have to sell Lakeside as is—half-painted walls and all.

"All finished?" Old Joe checked in the piece of equipment, eyeing her with suspicion. She assumed Joe, along with the rest of the town, had seen the incident at the concert.

"You have no idea." She scrawled her name on the slip. At least now she knew why her last name wasn't Dawson, when all along she'd assumed it was simply because her mom hadn't married her dad. So many pieces fell into place in ways that made her life even more fractured.

"I look forward to hearing your statement tomorrow." Joe cocked an eyebrow and leaned close. He reeked of stale coffee. "We all are."

Robyn left before he could say any more about the hearing. There was a lot for her to consider, and what she'd originally planned to say felt phony. She could go back to the statement Brad had written up for her, but as hurt as she was by Caleb, she refused to resort to following Brad's plan.

She approached the SUV, and Ginger quickly disconnected from her cell phone. Sadness swept over her at the thought of leaving her friend behind again, but she promised herself she'd keep their friendship intact. It'd be much easier than when she was a teenager, because this time she didn't have her mother to lie and connive and keep her from the people she loved.

"Let's walk." Ginger nudged her forward along the empty sidewalk. "I'm not taking you back to Lakeside where you can sit alone and feel miserable for the rest of the day."

"I'll be fine." Eventually. Robyn trained her focus on the clouds rolling into town. The day after tomorrow she'd be back on the beach where the surf would wash away her troubles or at least drown them out. Everything seemed better under the California sun. To think she'd almost surrendered to this dreary place, and for what? Good thing she figured out Caleb wasn't the right man for her before it was too late. How could she trust him after he'd kept that secret from her? Was he playing her, as Abby had suggested?

"I know you probably don't want to hear it, but I believe good will come out of this." Ginger pulled her umbrella out of her gold-colored tote. "I can't imagine how or what, but God will work this out for your benefit."

Robyn offered a weak smile. She knew in her head what Ginger said was true, but convincing her heart was another matter. She gripped the cross on her necklace to remind herself that she was loved and that she had a future, even if she didn't have a clue what it was. "I thought I'd finally found God's plan for me and that everything was as it should be. And now it's all changed. Everything I believed was wrong. I've been lied to by everyone."

"Not me."

"And for that I'm thankful." Drops splashed on her nose. She ducked under Ginger's umbrella and listened to the prickle of rain. "My own mother deceived me. How could she? Why wouldn't she tell me who my real father was?"

Ginger seemed to choose her words carefully. "In retrospect, what she did was bad, but maybe it was the best she could do for you at the time. The important thing was that Dan knew and still loved you."

She swiped a tear off her cheek. She was tired of crying, of feeling miserable and exhausted, but at least she now had proof of Dan's love. "Last night I read through the notes in his Bible. They were written after Brad and Abby's mom died. I was surprised the notes were all about me. He was waiting for me to come back—like the Prodigal." A smile tugged at her mouth, remembering the bittersweet moments she'd cherished alone after last night's disaster. "Not once did he ever mention that I wasn't really his daughter."

"That's because in his heart you were." Ginger's forehead wrinkled. "Do you have any idea why your mom told you Dan was your dad? Have you called to ask?"

"Not yet. I just couldn't bring myself to talk to her. But I thought about that all night, and the only thing I can figure is that they met after I was born. I assume that when they broke it off, he and I already had a bond that no one wanted to cut off." She rubbed a kink out of her tension-filled neck. "It's all guessing on my part, but I plan to have a long talk with my mom when the time is right. I'm so tired of all the confusion." *Thank You, Lord, for Dad's*

Bible. I'd be lost without it. She'd always think of Dan as her dad no matter what her birth certificate said. And at least now she knew why he hadn't come after her—he had no legal claim.

Ginger stopped under the awning outside the bakery and closed her umbrella. "I don't mean to pry, but how did you miss seeing that there was another man listed as the father?"

"I've never seen my birth certificate. Anytime I would have needed it, my mom was there. I can't think of a single instance I would have used it since I became an adult." She held up her hand and started ticking off her list. "I've never been out of the country. Haven't gotten married— and never will—"

"Stop. I have sympathy but no pity party. Never say never." Ginger ushered her inside, where the smell of fresh bread permeated the air.

Her mouth watered. She'd hardly eaten since Brad's revelation and was only too eager to order a bagel. After Mrs. Jones handed her a plate and a sorrowful smile, she grabbed a seat at the window. "Pity party aside, I think it's smart to steer clear of men. All men." She smeared a blob of cream cheese on the toasted side and took a bite.

"That's probably the best idea, at least for a while." Ginger set down her donut and reached across the table. "But I have to be honest. I still think Caleb is a good guy. For some reason, he didn't tell you what he knew, but maybe you should talk to him and at least find out why."

"Good guy? Are you kidding? None of it adds up."

"But remember, he's the one who told you himself that he was the cop. So he's not a liar or a coward. He must've had a good reason to wait, and you should hear him out."

She pinched the bridge of her nose. "I want to believe you, but I can't help thinking he used me to give a statement that would clear his name in front of the review board. What kind of man does that?"

"C'mon. Do you really believe he was using you? After all the time you spent together? After the way he devoted himself to fixing up Lakeside?" Ginger's eyes rounded, and she crumpled her napkin. "No one would do that on the miniscule chance that you'd take up for him and that your singular statement would sway the entire panel. That's a lot of ifs."

Robyn sat back and considered her friend's comments. Her assumption really did contain a lot of ifs and would take a master manipulator to pull off. "I want to believe that Caleb really cared about me and that the whole relationship wasn't a con, but I can't trust my own judgment right now. I thought it was the real thing, but how would I know? I don't know anything about love or relationships. But I do know that if he cared about me, then he would've told me as soon as he found out about my birth certificate."

"If you don't trust your judgment, then trust mine. I know people, and Caleb isn't the dirtbag that half the town is making him out to be—or the guy you think would create an entire scheme to sway the panel's recommendation." Ginger drilled into her with a convicting stare.

"I agree that people are wrong about him in regard to the accident, but I still don't know what I'm going to say tomorrow." She blew out a frustrated breath. She had a long night ahead of her. "Maybe I should skip the hearing and head back to California."

"You'd never forgive yourself. Remember, you were never doing this for Caleb. You were doing this for your dad. What would he say?"

"You're right." She tossed her napkin onto her plate and sat taller. "I'll figure something out. In the meantime, your job is to figure out how to sell Lakeside. Hopefully to someone who'll make it into something special."

Ginger's eyes turned down. "That means you're still leaving? You said that you wanted to settle down and make a home."

Of course that's what she wanted, but it wasn't going to happen. She finally understood the wanderlust her mother experienced, never able to stay after the loss of a job or a failed relationship. Sometimes it just didn't work out. Because even though she'd discovered she didn't know who her biological father was, she couldn't escape the fact that she would always be her mother's daughter.

Conversation rumbled through the tightly packed auditorium in the Pine Hollow Community Theater. People streamed in and filled every available seat, then proceeded to line the wall like sentinels ready to blockade the doors if Caleb moved an inch. Which he wouldn't, seeing as how even drawing a breath took an enormous amount of effort under the heavy weight of scrutiny.

Phil leaned over and spoke behind his hand. "Try to relax. Sitting like you're strapped to the electric chair isn't going to help."

"You try being on display." He scanned the sea of faces, hoping to see at least some that weren't scowling. He'd been instructed by Chief Warren to sit at a table at the front of the room in full sight of the crowd.

"I am—right here with you." Phil adjusted his tie and leaned back. "Time is your friend. One way or another, this will all be over in a few hours. By tomorrow afternoon, you'll have the board's recommendation and the chief's decision, and you can get on with your life."

He chewed on Phil's words—*one way or another.* He didn't like the sound of that since it implied the possibility of losing. How was it possible after so many hours of praying and searching that he hadn't fully surrendered? Was that why his gut ached at the thought of being forced out?

I will be with you in trouble.

The familiar Bible passage ran through his head, offering a brief reprieve from anxiety. Losing his job certainly qualified as trouble, but what was the worst that could happen? There was nothing God couldn't see him through. Although letting go of Robyn was going to be harder than letting go of the job.

Chief Warren positioned himself behind the podium and called the meeting to order. "We're here tonight to have a public hearing on the incident involving Officer Caleb Sloane and the death of Dan Dawson."

Shouts rang out across the room, and one or two brazen citizens lobbed verbal bombs at him. He glanced at Old Joe, who sat with the rest of the panel, wearing a smug expression. If this was any indication, Caleb was going down hard.

"We'll hear statements from the public. Form a line, and we'll get started." The chief stepped aside and ushered the first person to the microphone—a friend of Joe's, wearing a Remember Dan T-shirt.

Minute by torturous minute, Caleb listened to the testimony, which turned out to be a tribute to Dan rather than a diatribe on his handling of the incident. He whispered a prayer of thanks and somehow managed to keep his chin level.

Brad and Abby took their place in line, scorching him with their gazes. He braced himself for their attack. Robyn was conspicuously missing, which only intensified the uneasy feeling in his gut.

He shifted in his seat, trying to find the right balance between concerned and relaxed. The right balance between fear and faith. He settled for a stony expression, eyes raised to meet the crowd. Relief swept through him when Pastor Steve took his turn at the podium and highlighted the work Caleb had done in the community that reached deeper than simply patrolling the streets. After Pastor Steve had finished, Sue, the chief's secretary, spoke on his behalf. Then Dr. Nelson called for his dismissal. Mrs. Jones was next and spoke with conviction, telling the crowd to place the blame where it belonged—on Aaron.

Then it was Brad's turn. A high-pitched screech jolted the auditorium when he adjusted the microphone. "I appreciate all the nice words about my dad." His voice trembled, and he took a long pause. "Because he loved this town, I know he'd want what's best for Pine Hollow. How can the streets be safe when we have officers of the law acting against department guidelines? Caleb Sloane made the errant decision to pursue a vehicle in a high-speed chase, posing a threat to the citizens. He knew the department's no-pursuit policy and chose to ignore it. Pine Hollow is not safe with a renegade cop on the force, and I strongly advise the members of the panel to recommend the officer be immediately fired."

Caleb's insides liquefied. He shot a glance at Phil, who motioned for him to stay calm despite the murmurs of agreement in the crowd.

"My sister and I understand that Aaron Dirkson was primarily at fault, but we need to see everyone involved in the accident held accountable." Brad lanced him with a glare. "If it wasn't for Caleb Sloane, my sister and I would still have our father." His imploring gaze swept the room. "We'd *all* have him. Instead, the only thing we're left with are memories—and a call for justice."

At least half the crowd rose to their feet, cheering.

Caleb sank. Forget trying to look confident and car-ing. It wasn't enough. It never would be. He could only be thankful his father wasn't alive to see the shame brought by his poor decisions.

Abby's statement mirrored her brother's, only with tears that elicited sympathy from the crowd. She stopped several times to dry her eyes and eventually had to be led away from the podium.

The door at the back of the auditorium opened and closed with a clang. Caleb turned in time to see Robyn square her shoulders and head to the front of the room. People parted, most urging her to the head of the line.

His heart stuttered, but he wasn't sure if it was from anticipation of her denunciation of him or from the memories of their time together. He swallowed and willed himself to breathe. She couldn't possibly say anything worse than had already been said, especially since she didn't have a venomous bone in her body. But he knew with a desperate assurance that her words would cut the deepest.

The crowd stilled as Robyn adjusted the microphone. She drew a breath and directed her gaze at everyone but him. "I spent days trying to put together a statement that would reflect the way I feel, and then two days ago my world was upended—again." She cleared her throat and twined her fingers. "So I had to scrap what I'd planned and start over. Eventually I had to ask myself, what would Dad say?"

Brad crossed his arms, and even from the other side of the room, it was clear he took issue with Robyn's reference to their father.

She pulled a Bible from her purse and turned to the very end. "Thankfully, I discovered exactly what he would say." She ran her finger down the page, and a sad smile tugged at her lips. "Life has a funny way of turning out exactly the opposite of how you plan. The people you love the most might not love you back, and your hopes crumple up like yesterday's newspaper. But those are the times you learn who you are and what you believe. Do you believe in forgiveness or does it make you feel good to hold a grudge? Is life better with hope or disappointment?" She lifted her eyes from the Bible. "Mercy or judgment?"

Whispers spread through the room, and people nodded.

Robyn held up the Bible. "Those of you who knew my father already know the right thing to do." She looked at Old Joe. "Even if we're hurting, there's an honorable way to grieve." Slowly, she turned her gaze to Caleb with an expression mixed with sadness and regret. "And even if situations don't turn out like we want them to, life goes on."

He leaned forward, the ache in his heart expanding with each breath. Would she ever know how much he cared for her, how desperate he was to make things right?

Robyn looked away. "I'll be leaving tomorrow, but I hope that Pine Hollow finds healing. Now that I know I've been forgiven, I realize no matter how deep the pain that forgiveness is the greatest gift." She stepped back from the podium and blended into the crowd.

The people who'd been waiting in line drifted away. Chief Warren took the microphone and stole a glance at the panel. "I guess this concludes the public portion of the meeting."

Caleb stood, determined to find Robyn. He pressed past the groups huddled together and ignored the comments, good and bad. If he didn't find her now, he never would. He had to tell her how sorry he was—for everything. He wove through the people blocking the aisle until he came to the door, then he burst into the lobby and scanned the area until he spotted her near the entrance.

"Robyn, wait." He hustled to reach her. "Let me explain."

Tears glistened in her eyes. "I have to go. Please." Her voice warbled. "You don't know how hard this is after what happened."

"I'm so sorry."

"I understand, and I forgive you." She turned to leave and pushed open the glass door, never looking back.

He called after her, despite the swell of people in the foyer and despite his natural inclination to be private and guarded. "My feelings are real. They always have been."

But it was too late. She was gone.

Chapter Twenty-Two

Caleb slammed the air-hockey puck across the table and into the slot to score the final point. "Good game. Won't be long before you'll whip me at this." He reached out and shook hands with Rocky Lopez.

"There you are." Phil hurried across the recreation room, offering fist bumps to kids along the way. "I just heard the news."

He motioned his head toward the door. Once outside, he drew in a breath and basked in the sunshine. "It's finally over. I didn't think I'd ever get past that hearing." He meandered to the bench. "I heard from the chief first thing this morning. I start tomorrow."

"You don't sound excited." Phil loosened his tie.

"I am. Well, I'm more relieved than anything." He thanked God the crushing weight no longer pinned him down with worrisome thoughts and guilt, but his life still wasn't as it should be. Hopefully, Phil didn't press further since he wasn't up for a long discussion after such an exhausting month. He needed time to recover.

"I'm no expert, but I can see something's still wrong. Exhibit A, you're hanging out at the youth center when you should be chasing down the woman you love."

Caleb leaned forward on his knees and waved at the kids heading out to the badminton court. "What makes you think she wants to be chased?"

"All women want to be chased."

"Like you said, you're no expert." And neither was he, obviously. He'd bared his soul when Robyn walked out of the auditorium, yet she never looked back. The rejection carved a deep wound inside him, and the longer he went without seeing her, the more it festered. How could he have been so wrong about their relationship? For some crazy reason, he'd believed they'd already overcome the worst when she found out who he was. How had Brad's blowup changed her mind? She must have believed he'd used her, per Abby's accusation.

He'd been foolish to let himself get carried away with thoughts of forever, and now he had to face the consequences. Life without Robyn hardly seemed like a life at all. No more smiles and teasing or easy conversation. No more working quietly together. No more kisses.

"I might not know a lot about women, but even I can see you're letting a good one get away. She took a big blow when Brad told her about Dan. That's a lot of change for one person to go through in a short time." Phil sat next to him and shook his head. "She's hurting. But I'm sure she'll come around."

"She'll be gone by then." His throat tightened. Even his suspension from the force hadn't left him feeling this dejected and helpless. But what could he do other than let her go? He had no claim, no right to pursue her after she walked out.

"Not if you stop her."

"I'll bet she's already got Lakeside on the market—unless Brad is fighting it." He searched Phil's eyes for clues since he always knew more than he let on.

"No, man. I already told him the will is airtight." Phil waited until a couple strolled past before he continued. "Between you and me, he has some financial issues. He doesn't have the money to put up a fight, and he just wanted the proceeds from the sale of Lakeside to cover some of his debts."

"In that case, it looks like Robyn will be free to sell it right away. I hope she gets her asking price."

"In this market? Not likely." Phil leaned back and put his hands behind his head. "But it'll be a good deal for someone. I overhead Ginger talking to a potential buyer down at the café. Apparently, there are a few people sniffing around on it already, waiting for everything to settle. It's a nice piece of land."

Caleb didn't like the sound of it. After all that Robyn had been through, the last thing she deserved was to get cheated. They'd worked too hard and invested too much of themselves to let it go for less than it was worth. "I hate to see someone get cheap with her."

"I hear she just wants to get rid of it." Phil shot a sad look at him. "Too many memories, if you know what I mean."

"Are you pulling my chain?"

"Is it working?"

Caleb stood, irked. "I don't know what to think, and you're not helping. The whole thing is making me crazy, and it kills me to watch her leave."

"Then go to her. Make her stay." Phil pumped his fist in the air.

"I don't know how." He ran his hand through his hair, scraping up his courage and sending up a hurried prayer. Thoughts and ideas bombarded him, and he struggled to lay hold of one that made sense. "I already tried, and she wouldn't listen."

"Today's a new day, but tomorrow…" Phil sighed loudly. "Tomorrow she'll be gone. In fact, I overhead Ginger say she was picking her up in an hour to take her to the airport. What have you got to lose?"

"My pride, if she shoots me down again. But—"

"What good is pride…"

"If I'm having dinner with you. I know. Believe me, I know." Caleb patted his pocket for his keys. He had one chance left, and he wasn't going to miss it. He couldn't live with himself if he didn't at least try. "How long ago did you see Ginger?"

Phil glanced at his watch. "Hmm…I was at the café for a late lunch, then—"

"C'mon, how long?"

"Ten minutes, give or take. Hey, wait up," Phil called, "Are you going to Lakeside?"

"Yes, but first I have to find Ginger."

Robyn stuffed the last of her toiletries into her suitcase and zipped it shut, along with the dozens of memories she'd accumulated. She had to let them go or she'd be forced to live with regrets. Going back to California was the right decision. Back to a stable job and a not-so-stable mother who had a lot of explaining to do. Besides, Abby had told her on the phone this morning that she didn't see a relationship with her in the future, which meant Mom was— and would always be—her only family.

She rolled her luggage to the front room and glanced out the window. If only Ginger would hurry, it'd make the whole process easier, because the longer she waited the more doubt encroached. But what other choice did she have? Staying in Pine Hollow after what happened would be a huge mistake, and the thought of running into Caleb from time to time after what they'd almost had together filled her with sadness.

There had to be something left unfinished, something to keep her busy and occupy her thoughts. She'd already spent the morning going over every last inch of the property to make certain she hadn't missed any other important items of her father's for someone else to find. She'd also made arrangements for someone to come in and haul away the equipment in the boathouse. There was nothing left to do but wait.

Robyn pulled the door shut and locked it, determined not to peek through the window one final time. Mom had taught her never to look back. It was easier that way. Though clearly nothing about this move was easy.

The chime of her cell phone sent a squirrel scampering up a tree. She pulled the phone from her pocket and glanced at it. Mom. They'd spoken for the first time last night, and after the conversation—correction, argument—Robyn wasn't sure if she was up to dealing with another call. Then again, nothing would be resolved by holding a grudge.

"Hi, Mom."

"Just hear me out. I'm sorry I didn't tell you. I didn't think it mattered that Dan wasn't your real father because until that last argument, he treated you like his own. I see how it would be upsetting to find out like you did. I know I shouldn't have lied and said he didn't want you to come back, but I thought it best to finally leave that part of your life behind. It was getting too difficult to keep up the charade."

"It's okay, Mom. I forgive you." Robyn drew a pine-scented breath, deeply sad that it would be one of her last. She'd move on, and Lakeside Cabins would grow into a distant memory, as it had before. "It's just a lot to take

in right now. We can talk more when I get home." She
wanted peace with her mother, but she still wasn't up to
hearing more about how the man who was her biological
father never wanted to be part of her life. How when she
was an infant her mom met Dan, and Dan fell in love with
both of them—until Mom's wandering heart set them off
to find another path. At least Dan had continued to care
for her as best he could, and at least now, she knew who
she really was.

She hung up and offered a prayer of thanksgiving. Now
she could move on in truth, and that was as good a foun-
dation as anyone could hope for.

The wheels of her suitcase thumped over the flagstone
walkway as she headed for the clearing. The sound of
gravel crunching under tires broke through the quiet, and
moments later Ginger's SUV rounded the bend.

Thank You, Lord. Now I can put all this behind me.

She waved when Ginger climbed out. "I'm glad you're
here. I really appreciate the ride to Phoenix."

"Sorry I'm late. I was meeting with a client." Ginger
slammed the door and tucked her keys into her purse.

"That's fine. I'm ready to leave. The sooner, the better."

Ginger winced. "That might be a problem."

"Wait, I thought we were leaving right away." She
dragged her suitcase over the cinders and hefted it into
the back of the SUV. "I don't want to miss my flight."

"You can't pass up this opportunity." Ginger held up her
hands, her face suddenly animated. "I have a buyer who's
ready as soon as everything settles. We met right before I
got here, and he wants to have a look today."

Robyn folded her arms. "He made an offer before seeing it?"

"Everyone has seen Lakeside at one time or another.
Trust me. You want to be in on this deal."

"No, I don't. That's why I have you." Sorrow needled her, reminding her how much she hated to let Lakeside go. She couldn't handle seeing someone come in and take over. She'd planned to be long gone before that happened.

A black truck rounded the bend and pulled up in a cloud of dust.

Her heart banged against her rib cage—Caleb. She turned to Ginger, panicked. "What's he doing here? We should've already been gone."

He climbed out of his truck, his eyes filled with an intensity that made her tremble. "Thank God you're still here."

Ginger cleared her throat and stepped forward. "Robyn, meet your buyer."

"My buyer?" She glanced between them and turned the words over in her mind, trying to understand the implications. "I don't get it. You're the one buying Lakeside?"

"For asking price." Ginger nodded with a widening grin.

Caleb stepped closer, strong and confident. "Only if you approve the sale. I won't do it any other way."

She clutched her chest, willing her pulse to slow. She had so many competing questions but only one she could articulate. "How?"

"A friend at the credit union will help me work it out. I'm sure we can come to an arrangement."

"I'll just leave you two alone for a bit while I check on... something." Ginger backed away and then quickstepped to the house.

Robyn dared to look into Caleb's eyes, searching for answers. Searching for hope. He must have some feelings for her. After all, he'd come.

No. She couldn't allow herself to go there. This was a business transaction, plain and simple. He knew how much the land was worth and wanted to capitalize on it. Tonight she'd be on a plane, and tomorrow she'd be at the beach. Her old life would resume, and she would survive this ordeal intact, if not unscarred.

"Why?" Robyn asked. She wanted him to say something to contradict the person she was making him out to be, to reaffirm he was, instead, the man she'd been getting to know one disaster at a time. The man who'd walked with her through it all.

"Because I know a good thing when I see it." Caleb trapped her in his gaze, his eyes revealing more than his words.

"Even if it still needs a lot of work?"

He inched toward her and grazed her shoulders, his touch sending shock waves through her body. "I don't mind hard work because it makes the final result more valuable. I want to invest myself in something meaningful."

"But Lakeside? What could you possibly want with this old place?" Unbidden tears pricked her eyes. All the times she'd dared to imagine them together at the cabins came rushing back to her. Caleb had always seemed so right here, as though he belonged. As though they both did.

"I heard the current owner wants a buyer who'll make it into something special. Someone who'll love it back into shape. That's what I want to do—turn it into a small resort like it used to be." His thumb brushed away a tear she didn't know had fallen.

"But what if it's too big a project? It might not go as smoothly as you think." She reached up and cupped his hand against her cheek.

"I believe it's worth it, and I promise to do my best. And I always keep my promises." Caleb's eyes glittered in the sunlight. "Can you see it now? There should be a barbecue pit on the other side of the clearing."

"And there's room for more cabins." She offered a tentative smile, almost afraid to believe but more afraid not to.

"You're right about it being a big undertaking." Caleb leaned dangerously close, his sweet breath sweeping across her face. "And now that I have my old job back, I need just the right person to live here and be in charge." His voice deepened, and he caressed her cheek. "Do you know anyone who might be interested?"

"It has to be someone who loves Lakeside." She trembled as he fingered a lock of her hair.

"I agree."

"Someone who's like you. Someone who won't give up when things get hard." Her pulse quickened at the implication. Did he really mean he wanted her after everything that had happened? His very presence gave her the assurance she craved.

"Please stay." His soft gaze begged an answer. "I never meant to hurt you, and I can't imagine a life without you. Will you give us a chance?"

"So the whole thing wasn't a charade?"

"What does your heart say?" He stroked her arms.

"I want to believe you. I want to trust you." Robyn swallowed, trying to make room for hope. "I want to think that what was developing between us was real."

Caleb dipped his head to meet her gaze. "Everything is out in the open now. No more secrets. The dust has settled, and I'm still here."

For the first time since she'd come to Pine Hollow, confusion was replaced with clarity. The hearing was over, and Caleb *was* still here, asking her to be with him. No agenda, no suspicions. Only a deep longing they both shared.

"No more secrets?" Robyn searched his face and found truth.

"No more secrets. I want you to be able to count on me. The minute I know something, you will, too."

"How will you manage that?"

"Because I want you by my side."

Tears pricked her eyes, and a smile tugged at her mouth. "You still want me after everything we've been through?"

Caleb drew her close. "I do. Even more so, because I know what you're made of."

Through the fire, they'd both been tested. She'd seen him endure, even when the town was against him. Even when he thought she was against him. He was honorable and strong. Stable. Everything she needed, but was afraid to hope for. She clung to him. "I can't believe you're here."

"I know there's going to be things for us to work through, but I'm in it for the long haul, and I always will be." He pulled back far enough to gaze into her eyes. "I hope you will be, too."

"Yes." She nestled against his chest, feeling his heart-beat and warmth.

Caleb leaned down and drew her into a kiss that deepened with each breath. A kiss that erased her doubts and caused her to know she was right where she belonged. When he finally pulled back, a smile dawned on his face. A smile that spoke of shared dreams and a future.

"Thank you," she whispered. "For everything."

Caleb reeled her into a tight embrace. "I love you, Robyn. Welcome home."

Epilogue

One year later

Robyn stood at the foot of the steps, overwhelmed with gratitude. Had it only been a year since she'd first arrived, intent on setting Dad's affairs in order and leaving as soon as possible? At this point, the idea of ever giving up Lakeside Cabins was unthinkable. She'd finally found a home that wasn't just a place to sleep at night and store her stuff but a place where she truly belonged.

"A little higher." She motioned to Caleb, who raised the banner that hung over the porch a bit too high. "Lower. Wait, let me help you." She went up the stairs and started for the stool.

"Not on your life. No climbing for you." He held the corner of the banner just out of her reach, a grin teasing his lips.

"Don't you think you're being a little overprotective?" She pinched her fingers together. Her diamond wedding ring glinted in the sunlight, reminding her how much her life had changed since she'd come to Pine Hollow.

"It's what I do best." Caleb leaned down and grazed

her lips. "You're taking the next seven months easy, and I don't want to hear another word about it."

"Since when did I ever stop having something to say?" She fisted her hands on her hips.

"I only know one way to keep you quiet." He claimed her mouth with his and deepened the kiss until she was breathless.

Her heart lifted, anticipating a lifetime of Caleb's love. "I guess we'd better hurry before the guests arrive. If you hand me the hammer, I can take it from there."

"You're a hard woman to say no to." His eyes sparkled.

When they finished, they stood at the foot of the porch and gazed up at their work. "I can't believe it's finally happening. Grand reopening. The place looks better than it ever has." Emotion surged in her chest. If only Dad could have seen what'd they had accomplished over the past year.

"That's because we make a great team. I'm really looking forward to filling this place up. We got two more reservations this morning." Caleb slung his arm around her and squeezed.

An SUV rounded the bend in a cloud of dust. Ginger climbed out and tottered over the grass in spiky heels with her cell phone in one hand and a casserole dish in the other. She gazed over the property, eyes wide. "The landscaping is fabulous. When you said you were putting in a rock garden, I had my doubts, but I'm impressed. The fountain is a nice touch, too."

Robyn took the casserole dish and walked with Ginger to the table at the front of the main house. "If you look past cabin four, you can see where we broke ground for the next two units. You really should come out more often." She winked at her friend.

"Now that you had the road fixed, you can count on it." Ginger nudged her with a playful elbow before her face turned somber. "I'm sorry to hear your mom isn't coming today."

Her heart dipped at the mention of her mother. "I'm sorry for that, too, but she promised she'd be out for the baby." She restacked the napkins and fixed a paperweight over them. "But the important thing is that we've moved past all the anger, and she even told me how to get in touch with my biological father."

Ginger's eyebrows drew tight. "Are you ready for that?"

"Caleb and I are still praying about it. Only God knows what the future holds, so I'm going to leave it up to Him." And for the first time in years, she was truly at peace with it. After all, if God could see her through the past year, she knew He'd hold her hand through the rest. He'd already given her everything she wanted—a real home…and a husband to share it with.

Guests arrived, offering food, hugs and congratulations—both for the baby and the grand reopening—until the property was filled with people and laughter. Smoke and the smell of burgers and roasted corn wafted from the barbecue, where Pastor Steve tended the grill wielding an oversize spatula.

"You're going to need a bigger parking lot." Phil gave Robyn a side hug and Caleb a handshake. "I'm going to check out the desserts." He donned his sunglasses before sauntering over to the table next to Ginger.

"Do you see what I'm seeing?" Robyn nestled into the crook of Caleb's arm and listened to their friends fumble through a bit of conversation and a few awkward laughs.

"I have to admit that Phil's making the slowest move in the history of dating. I don't know how many times he's started to ask her out, then backed off." He shook his head.

Robyn narrowed her eyes at her husband. "He has?"

"I keep telling him to go for it."

She settled into his embrace. "I'm glad you didn't take that long."

"I couldn't wait for you to be Mrs. Sloane." He rested his chin on top of her head.

"All right you lovebirds. I think it's time to pray." Pastor Steve set the platter of food on the table as people gathered. "Lord, we come before You this glorious day to give thanks. Thank You for friends and family, for food and fellowship. For all Your blessings, we give You praise."

A chorus of amens went up from the group. Mrs. Jones directed everyone to form a line on each side of the table, then file over to the newly installed covered picnic area. The festive mood continued, and even Chief Warren joined in. The change in his relationship with Caleb was astonishing and could only be attributed to prayer.

Another car rounded the bend and came to a stop at the edge of the property. A sharp breath punctured Robyn. "It's Abby." She clutched her chest. "I haven't heard from her in months." Not since the birthday card she'd sent to Abby in the spring, which Abby had vaguely acknowledged. Now that they knew they weren't even half sisters, she understood the chances of them forming a lasting bond were slim. Or nonexistent. And though she'd come to terms with the realization, she still mourned the friendship they'd had as small children.

Caleb grabbed her hand. "I'll come with you."

Together, they walked to the car just as Abby climbed out and offered a simple smile. "I heard you were having a shindig."

Robyn drew a sturdy breath as she tried to read Abby's intentions. "It's a grand reopening of Lakeside Cabin Resort."

Abby's gaze swept the property. Slowly, she nodded.

"Dad would've loved this." She closed the door to her car. "I hope you don't mind my showing up uninvited."

"You're always welcome." She took a tentative step closer. "I'm really surprised…and happy to see you."

"It's taken me a while to get over some things, and of course, Brad hasn't been any help—"

"How is he?" Robyn had prayed for him daily, hoping one day his heart would soften.

"He's digging his way out of his problems." Abby waved her off. "I decided I can't always listen to him." She opened the door, and the two most adorable twin boys Robyn had ever seen clambered out of the vehicle. With curly brown hair and rounded cheeks, they both had the stark blue eyes that seemed to run in the family. "I also decided it was time for my kids to meet Aunt Robyn."

Aunt Robyn? She could definitely get used to that.

Instantly, she bent down and scooped the children into an embrace. "I've been so anxious to meet you both." She inhaled the scent of dirt and bubble gum—exactly how four-year-old boys should smell. Tears trickled down her cheeks, and she didn't bother to wipe them away. Finally, she drew back and whispered a thank-you to Abby before ushering them toward the food. "When the kids are done eating, you and I can show them all the best hiding spots and trees to climb."

A slow smile spread across Abby's face. "I'd like that." She urged her kids toward the table laden with treats.

Caleb palmed Robyn's shoulders, then wheeled her back against his chest. "Looks like our prayers have been answered."

"God has been so kind to us." She snuggled into her husband and marveled at the warmth and friendship in their gathering.

In that moment, her heart was filled. Filled with love

for her husband and unborn child. Filled with the joy of their promising future. And most of all, it was filled with the one thing she'd always craved most and now knew in abundance—the love of her Father.

* * * * *

Dear Reader,

Thank you for spending time with me in the fictional town of Pine Hollow, nestled in the beautiful mountains of northern Arizona. I hope you enjoyed the journey with Caleb and Robyn as they worked to overcome situations that were often out of their control but completely in God's hands. During seasons of rejection, pain or the loss of a loved one is when we'll find God at work behind the scenes. He desires to take even the worst circumstances of our lives and bring healing and restoration.

It is my hope that you will prayerfully right those relationships that God has been nudging you about, and consider how to apply forgiveness and mercy in your daily life. Don't allow the hurts of the past to keep you from God's amazing plan for you today. I pray you experience God in a fresh new way, and are open to the love and attention He wants to lavish on you simply because you are the treasure of His heart.

This is true love.

Blessings,
Georgiana Daniels

Questions for Discussion

1. Robyn and her father were estranged until it was too late to restore their relationship. How do you think this affected her decision-making and her view of relationships?

2. Caleb was faced with the possibility of losing his job. Have you faced a job loss? How did it affect your faith?

3. When Robyn and Ginger reunite after several years apart, they fall back into their friendship right away. Have you reunited with a long-lost friend? Did you have to overcome hard feelings or was it as though time hadn't passed?

4. Caleb harbored a big secret in order to protect Robyn from Brad. Have you ever had to keep a secret for someone else's benefit? How did it affect you?

5. Phil keeps prodding Caleb to tell Robyn everything. Have you had a friend who pushes you toward truth? Is this a characteristic you seek in your closest friends? In what situations have you been this type of friend?

6. Robyn is desperate to know if her father forgave her. She felt rejected by him, and until the end she didn't know why. In what situations have you felt rejected by your family, and how did you handle those relationships going forward?

7. Caleb realizes he's falling for Robyn but fears she will reject him once she knows all about him. Have you

feared rejection if someone were to know the full truth about you? How did you overcome it?

8. Robyn is willing to do almost anything to restore her relationship with her siblings. What lengths have you gone to in order to restore a family relationship?

9. The people of Pine Hollow are divided and want justice after Dan's death. What kinds of issues have divided your town and how were they resolved? What does justice mean to you?

10. Brad and Abby are cruel to Robyn because she had caused a wedge in their family and yet she received Lakeside as an inheritance. Were their feelings justified? When have you experienced this level of jealousy and anger, and how did you get over it?

11. Abby felt sibling rivalry when she was old enough to realize Robyn was also Dan's daughter, not just a child who came to visit each summer. Have you experienced sibling rivalry? Did it resolve as you got older, or do you continue to struggle?

12. After the accident, Caleb stayed away from the church for a while because he didn't want to face Dan's friends. Have you ever stayed away from the church for a season, and what finally brought you back?

13. Caleb struggles between knowing he made the best decision he could at the time and guilt over the horrific outcome. Think of a time you did what you felt was right but the unintended consequences hurt someone else. How was the issue resolved?

14. Robyn feels duped when she discovers who Caleb is, and feels she should have seen this coming after all the bad experiences her mother had with men. Have you felt that way about someone you were starting to have feelings for? How did you handle the situation?

15. Robyn reveals her belief that Dan would want the town to show mercy to Caleb. What does mercy mean to you? In what situation have you been given mercy, or granted mercy to someone else?

REQUEST YOUR FREE BOOKS!

2 FREE INSPIRATIONAL NOVELS
PLUS 2
FREE
MYSTERY GIFTS

Love Inspired

YES! Please send me 2 FREE Love Inspired® novels and my 2 FREE mystery gifts (gifts are worth about $10). After receiving them, if I don't wish to receive any more books, I can return the shipping statement marked "cancel." If I don't cancel, I will receive 6 brand-new novels every month and be billed just $4.49 per book in the U.S. or $4.99 per book in Canada. That's a saving of at least 22% off the cover price. It's quite a bargain! Shipping and handling is just 50¢ per book in the U.S. and 75¢ per book in Canada.* I understand that accepting the 2 free books and gifts places me under no obligation to buy anything. I can always return a shipment and cancel at any time. Even if I never buy another book, the two free books and gifts are mine to keep forever.

105/305 IDN FVV7

Name _____ (PLEASE PRINT)

Address _____ Apt. #

City _____ State/Prov. _____ Zip/Postal Code

Signature (if under 18, a parent or guardian must sign)

Mail to the **Harlequin® Reader Service:**
IN U.S.A.: P.O. Box 1867, Buffalo, NY 14240-1867
IN CANADA: P.O. Box 609, Fort Erie, Ontario L2A 5X3

**Are you a subscriber to Love Inspired books
and want to receive the larger-print edition?
Call 1-800-873-8635 or visit www.ReaderService.com.**

* Terms and prices subject to change without notice. Prices do not include applicable taxes. Sales tax applicable in N.Y. Canadian residents will be charged applicable taxes. Offer not valid in Quebec. This offer is limited to one order per household. Not valid for current subscribers to Love Inspired books. All orders subject to credit approval. Credit or debit balances in a customer's account(s) may be offset by any other outstanding balance owed by or to the customer. Please allow 4 to 6 weeks for delivery. Offer available while quantities last.

Your Privacy—The Harlequin® Reader Service is committed to protecting your privacy. Our Privacy Policy is available online at www.ReaderService.com or upon request from the Harlequin Reader Service.

We make a portion of our mailing list available to reputable third parties that offer products we believe may interest you. If you prefer that we not exchange your name with third parties, or if you wish to clarify or modify your communication preferences, please visit us at www.ReaderService.com/consumerschoice or write to us at Harlequin Reader Service Preference Service, P.O. Box 9062, Buffalo, NY 14269. Include your complete name and address.

LI13

All Laura White wants is a second chance.
Will she find it in Cooper Creek?

Read on for a preview of
THE COWBOY'S HEALING WAYS.

The door opened, bringing in cool air and a few stray drops of rain. The man in the doorway slipped off boots and hung a cowboy hat on a hook by the door. She watched as he shrugged out of his jacket and hung it next to his hat.

When he turned, she stared up at a man with dark hair that brushed his collar and lean, handsome features. He looked as at home in this big house as he did in his worn jeans and flannel shirt. His dark eyes studied her with curious suspicion. She'd gotten used to that look. She'd gotten used to people whispering behind their hands as she walked past.

But second chances and starting over meant wanting something new. She wanted to be the person people welcomed into their lives. She wanted to be the woman a man took a second look at, maybe a third.

Jesse Cooper took a second look, but it was a look of suspicion.

"Jesse, I'm so glad you're here." Granny Myrna had returned with a cold washcloth, which she placed on Laura's forehead. "It seems I had an accident."

"Really?" Jesse smiled a little, warming the coolness in dark eyes that focused on Laura.

"I pulled right out in front of her. She drove her car off the side of the road to keep from hitting me."

Laura closed her eyes. A cool hand touched the gash at her hairline.

"Let me see this."

She opened her eyes and he was squatting in front of her, studying the cut. He looked from the gash to her face. Then he moved and stood back up, unfolding his long legs with graceful ease. Laura clasped her hands to keep them from shaking.

A while back there had been an earthquake in Oklahoma. Laura remembered when it happened, and how they'd all wondered if they'd really felt the earth move or if it had been their imaginations. She was pretty sure it had just happened again. The earth had moved, shifting precariously as a hand touched her face and dark eyes studied her intently, with a strange mixture of curiosity, surprise and something else.

Will Jesse ever allow the mysterious Laura
into his life—and his heart?

Pick up THE COWBOY'S HEALING WAYS
by Brenda Minton,
available in February 2013 from Love Inspired.